Olivia Gaines

Also by Olivia Gaines

The Short Stories

Two Nights in Vegas
The Basemen of M. McGee
A Letter to My Mother
The Perfect Man
A New Mommy for Christmas
Beneath the Well of Dawn
The Bounty: Revenge Can be a Bitch
The Bounty: Lizzie's Vengeance
North to Alaska
My Mail Order Wife

The Blakemore Files

Being Mrs. Blakemore
Shopping with Mrs. Blakemore
Dancing with Mr. Blakemore

The Novels

A Few More Nights
Friends with Benefits
The Cost To Play
A Menu for Loving
Courting Guinevere
Loving Words
Vanity's Pleasure

A Menu For Loving

Olivia Gaines

Davonshire House
Publishing

Davonshire House Publishing
PO Box 9716
Augusta, GA 30916

© 2015 Olivia Gaines, Cheryl Aaron Corbin

Copy Editor: Rachel Bishop
Line Editor: Teresa Thompson Blackwell
Special Promotions: Pilgrim Soap Company, Augusta, GA
Cover: koougraphics
Olivia Gaines Make Up and Photograph by Latasla Gardner Photography

ISBN-13: 978-0692380062
ISBN-10: 069238006X

Printed in the United States of America
1 2   3   4   5   6   7   10   9 8

First Davonshire House Publishing February 2015

DEDICATION

For every woman who still believes in the happily ever after, even if your family is nucking futs.

Olivia Gaines

Easy reading is damn hard writing.- Nathaniel Hawthorne

ACKNOWLEDGMENTS

Thank you to my online community and network of writers.

An extra special thank you to my bibliophiles who keep my nose to the grindstone.

And thank you, for spending some time in my magical world.

Write On!

Est 2009

Augusta Writers

This is Jennifer and Tony Peay

Come on inside and read about how they fell in love.

Olivia Gaines

Setting out the appetizer...

It could have possibly been the most desperate night of her life. Mix desperation with an extremely loud hormonally charged ticking time clock and the perfect recipe for disaster is concocted. When all of that is stirred up with a certain type of situational insanity that takes over a human brain, it can make for a crazy night. Gently fold in a major life event, which is suddenly aerated by adding another ridiculous rite of passage and even the sanest woman can turn into a simmering, bubbling idiot. No, it is not the simple life events like graduating high school, going to college or getting married that can drive a person nuts. It's the life events that transpire like a class reunion.

Ahhh, the class reunion. It is the one point in a person's life where the people who *really* know who you are gathered in one room to continue to judge you. It only intensifies the futility of your existence when it is realized that since you graduated high school, you didn't go to a four-year college, and are single again with no children. It would even be semi-acceptable if you were a single parent, at least that way you would have a story to tell and there was undeniable proof that at one point, you were getting some. No matter how brief or short the copulated activity that created your burden of proof, you got some – from someone other than yourself.

Jennifer Taylor's story was short. After graduating high school, she enrolled in culinary school and studied at *Le Cordon Bleu* in Atlanta. She was lucky upon graduation to get a cooking gig as a private chef for a famous Atlanta rapper turned producer. That position led to a cushy gig in Los Angeles for a prominent high profile booking agent, which sounded glamorous, but in reality, she was stuck in the kitchen. Eight years of stuck in the kitchen. Now, she was stuck going to a reunion that she had no interest in attending. Thanks to a meddlesome father who, for the damndest reason, saw fit to open all the mail that came in the house. Everything except his own mail, that is. Those bills, he swore, were misunderstandings. The businesses, he claimed, misunderstood the idea that he planned to pay them before he died. Jennifer was starting to believe that after this reunion, his death by her hand was imminent.

Her father, God bless his cantankerous, manipulative, sneaky, underhanded soul, was so desperate for grandkids that he accepted the reunion invite and even paid her fees. Jennifer was no dummy. She knew what he was up to. He figured, since her sister Gloria was gay, that she was his only chance of ever being called "G-Pop." He completed her registration hoping she would find a man. At this point, her dad didn't even care if she married the dude. He just wanted some grandkids to spoil. Family is weird that way. Her father spoiled her and now that she was a very busy adult, he needed someone new to dote on. He gave her specific instructions that she really had no intention of heeding. "Girl, go out there, find a man and make me a granddaddy!" He patted her on the head just as he would when he dropped her off to school each morning, followed by a kiss to the top of her head and a gentle nudge forward. Johnny Taylor, not related to the singer, he always said, nudged her again to

4

make some changes in her life and to get out there.

And there she stood. In front of the Marriott, staring at the double glass doors. Out there. Her reflection in the clinging royal blue wrap dress staring back at her. Tonight she wore her hair down, since she seldom had an opportunity to do so in her line of work. The naturally loose curls were straightened and hung about her shoulders. She tossed them back as she inhaled deeply and made her way through the main doors.

A bar.

A bar with liquor.

Straight liquor.

Strong liquor.

Liquid courage.

"Thank you," she said as she looked up at the ceiling, hoping a higher power had heard her cry.

The heavy pub style door opened into a moderately lit, run of the mill hotel lobby bar. At the corner of the bar was the cliché traveling salesman who was passing out business cards and trying to pimp whatever product still required a physical salesperson. In the corner was the proverbial married man, waiting on his Saturday night rendezvous. Jennifer took a slow, deliberate step towards the bar with wide eyes that scanned the room. Four. There were four potential men in the room who could easily be her date for the night.

Candidate one. *He has potential.* Tall, athletic, cocoa skin, and a receding hairline that started at his ears. He flashed her a grin. *Oh! No!* The brother was missing his two front teeth. She didn't smile back.

Candidate two. Nervous. Twitchy. *Married.* He had nice eyes. The nice eyes did not compensate for the wolfish grin or the fact she saw him remove the wedding ring and slip it into his pocket. Nope.

Candidate three looked at her and licked his lips. This was done simultaneously as he dropped his hand to his crotch to indicate he and his little friend were ready to play. The man stood up. Jennifer's eyes got wide and she almost turned to head out the door, but gentleman number four glanced her way.

He is hot. The hair was a bit longer than she would have liked, but she was in a bind. That meddlesome father of hers had paid for her and a plus one, and she was currently hovering at minus one. If things continued as they were currently progressing, this class reunion would be negative one.

"Hi," she said to candidate number four.

"Hello," he responded.

She stood beside him as he sipped at his drink and he stared at her reflection through the mirror behind the bar. He cut his eyes at her, giving her a sideways glance, waiting for her to state her business. It was obvious she was gathering her courage, so he turned on the bar stool to face her.

"Are you married?"

"No," he stated calmly.

"Waiting for someone?" She asked pleasantly.

"No," he answered as he kept his eyes trained on hers. He did not allow his eyes to rake over her body, which put her at ease. "To answer your next questions, I am straight, single, not engaged. I am here to have a drink."

He could see her physically relax somewhat as her hand lifted the hair from her neck to drape it over her shoulder. "I am in a bind," she started slowly. "My ten-year class reunion is in that main ballroom. I don't have a date and I cannot bear to walk through those doors alone. So, if you are okay with it, I need you to be my man for the night."

She had his undivided.

"Your man?" The smile he gave her went all the way up to his eyes, creating little crow's feet at the corners.

"Yes, my man. And we have been seeing each for six months. We are madly in love and you can't keep your hands off me."

His eyes still remained on her face as he slowly rose from the stool to stand toe-to-toe with her. As he uprighted himself, he turned out to be a good deal more man than it appeared as he sat on that stool. Surprisingly, he picked up his drink, knocked it back in one swallow and reached for her hand. "Let's do it," he said.

Jennifer stuttered, "You are agreeing to do this?"

"Yep. It's far more interesting than what I had planned for the evening, which was two more drinks and ordering a movie in my room," he told her as his fingers closed over hers. Warm fingers that gave her hope. "Lead the way."

"I'm Jennifer," she told him as he opened the bar door that lead to the main lobby.

"Tony," he said, offering her his elbow.

"Thank you, Tony," she told him and placed her arm in his.

"You may be thanking me, too, soon," he said dryly. It was the way he said it that made Jennifer stop in her tracks.

"Hold up, Tony. When I said you can't keep your

hands off me, I mean, you know, moderate PDA. No lewdness, groping, or crazy stuff, okay?" Her eyes scanned his face, searching for a modicum of comprehension at her words. She spotted a flicker of something else that was registering on his face.

There are moments and then there are moments between a man and woman that speak volumes. Tony was about to create one of those instances. As he faced her in the narrow hallway under the grand staircase, he said something to her with utter conviction in his words that would be the start of a change in her life.

"Kiss me and tell me you love me," he said with a sultry need in his voice.

"What?" she said and took a step back.

"Exactly!" he told her and moved closer, lifting a strand of her hair and pushing it behind her ear. "If this is going to work, you have to get comfortable with my touch, my hands on you and being affectionate with me in front of all of your classmates. Let's practice."

He moved closer and placed his arms about her waist. "Jennifer, tell me you love me, then kiss me like you mean it."

Tony's eyes were deep brown with long lashes that seemed almost too perfect to belong to a man. His hair was black with evenly tapered sideburns, which faded into a five o'clock shadow. It was a bonus that he was already in a dark suit that seemed to drape over muscles begging to be freed. Jennifer felt alive as sparks shot through her fingers and she reached for his hair, toying with a loose strand. Her fingers ran across his bottom lip, and she looked at it with a hunger. Slowly, her eyes lifted to meet his, as he watched her with a curious stare, waiting to see how well she could lie.

"Tony," she said huskily and she brought her lips to his, pressing hard against his mouth as she mumbled the words, "I love you so much for being here for me."

He wrapped his arms around her waist and deepened the kiss, but only briefly before pulling away. "Let's go have some fun, Jen."

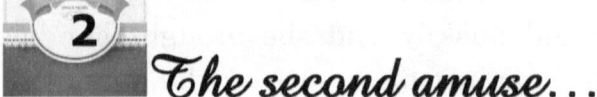

The second amuse...

It could not be denied that Tony, the Man of the Hour, had a warped sense of fun. In less than three minutes, he began what became the start of the most interesting year of Jennifer Taylor's life. There was no denying two things about the man. One, he had a roguish sense of humor with a quick wit. Two, he was deliciously wicked. Both of which she found appealing to her palate.

Several times during the course of the evening's activities, Jennifer had to turn her back to stifle her shock, her laughter and downright amusement at her date's antics. He was serving up small plates full of wonders that sent her mind into overdrive. The fun started immediately after they checked in at the registration desk and nature called him away for a quick visit, which, of course, left her alone inside the door.

Catherine McCaulley, the class busybody, gossipmonger and all around bad spirit, was also at the door to greet her solo arrival. "Jennifer Taylor, as I live and breathe. Look at you, girl! Still skinny and cute. Are you alone?"

"No, my..." she didn't know what to call him, "... date will be back soon." There must have been blood in the water because the other sharks swam over, ready to feed upon the carrion they were certain that Catherine was going to leave. Rosie Muńez, Reba Foley and Dorothy Wasshername sidled over, all grins. Evil grins. Sporting those 'I am going to eat your brains for breakfast' grins.

In unison, like the Weird Sisters in *Macbeth*, all three

asked, "Jennifer, where's your date?"

She held up her finger, her elbow almost at a perfect 90-degree angle, to point in the general direction of the men's room, but gasped as she felt a warm mouth close over it. Tony had snuck up behind her and was suckling at her finger. When she was able to finally extract it from his mouth with a very loud pop goes the weasel sound, he continued to shock her by saying, "I was wondering where you had gotten off to with yo' fine ass."

Trying to hide her shock, she said, "You know I can never be too far from your side, Tony," as she turned to face him.

His grin was wide and his eyes were sparkling, as if he was challenging her to play along with his little game of chance. "That's what I'm talking about. Give Daddy some sugar, baby," he said with laughter in his eyes.

"Daddy?" she asked with her eyebrows arched and mouth slightly ajar.

He winked at her twice, licked his bottom lip and pulled her so close to him that she could almost hear the systolic and diastolic pressure hit his aortic walls. "Girl, don't say it like that in public, you know what it does to me. We'll have to cut this reunion short while I reacquaint you with an old friend and your best buddy," he said as his hand slid down her waist to rest on her butt cheek.

The feeble attempt to not smile at his antics was halted by his mouth coming for hers, but he stopped to ask, "Are these your friends, Jen? Intros please, ladies," he said to the witches.

"Catherine," she said as she stuck out her hand.

"Reba, like the country music star," she told him as

she extended her hand.

Dorothy and Rosie nearly knocked each other over trying to introduce themselves. "Pleasure," he said as he smiled at them but turned his attention back to Jennifer.

"Speaking of pleasure, you sexy breath stealer, the more I think about it, the less I want to be down here instead of up in our room. How long do you have to stay at this thing?"

"Tony, we just got here," she pretended to whine as her hands stroked the fabric of the arms on his jacket sleeves.

"I know, baby, but I want you all to myself," he said as he kissed her on the collarbone. The witches all moaned as they watched his teeth nip at the skin on her shoulder.

"Is that Tony P?" someone yelled across the room, which distracted him for a second, and four football players came over to greet him. The largest of the entourage of no-necked men addressed Tony. "You didn't go to school here."

"Man, you're the enemy," another said jokingly.

What does the P stand for?

While the guys pulled him away, Jennifer tried to listen. Apparently, Tony had played football for a rival school. The constant buzzing about her ears was distracting as the witches of Piney Brook High chatted away at her, pelting her with questions about Tony. "Ladies, why are you all asking so many questions about my man?" Which brought them all to heel.

"Baby, I'm going to the bar. I'll bring you something back to wet that sexy whistle," he said as he followed the guys toward the bar area. Like a second thought of intuition tapped him on the shoulder, he came back to her, and pulled her close again. "I think you forgot my kiss. Give Daddy his sugar, baby."

She could not help but grin like a fool as she leaned forward to kiss him, only to be lifted from her feet as his mouth slanted over hers again and again while he turned her in a slow circle. His tongue slipped inside her mouth, playing with her own until he finally put her back on solid ground. She was slightly dizzy and wobbly on her feet. "Be back in a minute to follow that up with something even wetter," he said as he winked at her.

Catherine said what Jennifer was thinking. "What he is planning to happen in your room later seems a helluva lot more fun that what is happening down here."

But it wasn't true. It was so far from the truth that as the evening progressed, he became more amusing. She whispered to Tony in a low voice, "You are really enjoying yourself aren't you?"

"Baby, you have no idea how much fun I'm having," he told her as his hand roamed across her butt cheek. The evening's activities were like a big theme park for her date, who seemed to find a great deal of delight in his choices of ways to shock and tickle her.

The first large enjoyment came when a song that she loved came on and she wanted to dance. "I dance like the white boy that I am, you are not getting me on the dance floor," he said adamantly. "I am not going out there looking like an unseen puppet master is trying to teach me to be Elvis!"

"That is shocking, considering you have been channeling you inner homeboy for the past few hours," she told him as she ran her hand up his arm.

"You aren't kidding. When I saw you turn around in the dress and I caught a glimpse of *dat ass*, I got all crunk. You even have a little mini-shelf back there," he chuckled as he rested his hand on top of her butt.

Jennifer found herself genuinely laughing and even enjoying herself the more he talked. The way he played with words and his word choices had her nearly hanging on his every syllable. Something that he did not let go unnoticed. He grinned as he pulled her in close. "You keep looking at me like you want some of this...." This only made her smile bigger. All of that occurred in the first hour of meeting him.

Throughout the next two hours, she also found herself appreciating his company. They were so in sync that, for a minute, it almost felt real. She fed him appetizers and finger foods as he licked her digits to get every drop. He, in turn, gazed into her eyes when he spoke to her, and randomly, during her responses to him, he would kiss her for no reason. It was an odd trust of sorts and she wanted to test how much of what she was experiencing was real. She wanted to at least dance once with him. Curiosity was propelling her into a random kitchen to heat a pot of water just to watch it boil. Jennifer wanted to be in his arms and move with him. "Tony, I would like to dance," she whispered in his ear.

"I am not any good at it, but I can two step," he told her as his finger rolled across her shoulder blade.

"Fair enough, if you are willing, let me guide you and show you some basic dance moves." She pulled him by the hand to the dance floor as *Dark Horse* started. Her hands around his waist, she leaned into his strength, whispering in his ear, "Dancing is just like making love. We match each other's movement. When I move forward with my right, you step back with your left." She counted off to three and he stepped backwards. "Feel my hips against yours, rock with me."

When the tempo of the music changed, she told him, "Listen and feel the undertones of the beat." He followed, swaying, rocking, and moving with her. "That's good. Now double up on that move." Tony rocked with her. "Sit back in it, during this soft part. Move just your shoulders," she said. "Good, the tempo is about to change, ready?" she asked.

"Now you take over," she told him.

Tony's hands came up, cupping her face as he kissed her again while moving his hips in a basic rhythm, which she matched and followed along with. She pulled away from the kiss and gazed into his eyes as she followed his movement with her hips. They were totally in sync. If it wasn't real, it certainly felt like it.

Someone yelled, "Get a room!"

The song ended and he stopped, simply staring at her. "That's a good idea and I have one." He pulled her by her hand towards the door.

"Wait, where are we going?"

"To my room," he said as they rounded the corner to the elevators. He pressed impatiently on the button for the car to arrive, pulling her inside when it did.

"What makes you think this is going to happen?" she asked.

Tony unfastened the buttons on his jacket, allowing the fabric to fall open. He pulled her closer to him, yanking her hand towards his body and opening the jacket, placing her hand on the reason logic was leaving them both. "I have been making out with you for damn near three hours and I am so turnt up right now, telling me no would be cruel and unusual punishment."

The elevator stopped and he stepped out. Jennifer leaned against the back of the elevator walls, staring at him, questioning what she was doing. Wanting him yet knowing it was not a smart move, but it had been so long since she had enjoyed the touch of a man. Tony extended his hand to her. "Come with me, Jen, let me make love to you."

Uncertain legs led her through the doors as she slipped her hand into his to be guided to his room. The ideas he gently laid in the dish of her mind were adorned with sexy ribbons, covered with chocolate, dripping with lust, and she wanted to sample everything on the platter. Jennifer knew she must have left half of her common sense in the elevator with her inhibitions because he basically screwed the rest of it out her head.

Fine as caviar...

If there was one thing Jennifer's father had instilled in her about men, it was this: a man will tell you everything you want to hear, but his actions will tell you who he is. For three hours, Tony P – and she was sad to admit that she didn't know what the P stood for, let alone his last name – had wooed her with his words. Three solid hours of hands-on stimulation followed by soft verses whispered in her ear reeled her in like the Sirens luring her to the jagged rocks. She was now in his room, behind a closed door with no one but the two of them. His words had brought her here and she only hoped that she would not be disappointed by his actions.

She was not. As easily as he spent three hours wooing her and playing boyfriend, he spent the next three hours backing up his words by being her very real lover. His conversation became limited and he only spoke enough to ensure her pleasure and to provide subtle instructions.

Tony moved with confidence as he opened the door to his room, hanging his coat on the back of a chair. The cell phone in his inner coat pocket was removed as he showed it to her and pushed the off switch. "Your turn," he said as he placed his phone inside of the nightstand drawer. Jennifer turned her cell phone off and attempted to put it inside of her purse, but accidently knocked it over, spilling all the contents on the floor.

"I'm sorry. I'm nervous," was thrown into the air in Tony's direction with a weak smile.

"Don't be," he said as he walked over to her, helping her up from the floor. "It will be just like dancing," he winked at her as he pulled the ties on the wrap dress, allowing the fabric to hang loosely as he removed the blue material from her body. It impressed her that he had not slung it to the floor, but gently draped it over the back of the chair. With ease and care, he removed every stitch of her clothing and placed it upon the chair as well, leaving Jennifer naked, vulnerable and wearing nothing but a weak smile.

"Undress me, Jen," he said in a way that was more asking than telling as her nervous fingers began to unbutton his shirt. The soft cotton fabric slid over his broad shoulders, revealing the wide chest covered in muscles. Instead of draping the shirt over the other chair in the room, she walked it to the closet and hung it on a hanger. Tony had not moved from his spot. His eyes filled with hunger as he watched her move.

Her hands went to his belt buckle, tugging at the leather, releasing the snap of his pants, then tugging at the metal tab, listening to the teeth release on the zipper. She tapped at his thigh, indicating he needed to step from the pants that she also took and hung in the closet. When she returned, he had removed his socks and shoes and stood before her, bare, beautiful and ready to move forward.

"Wow," she said as she tried to catch her breath.

The second thing that impressed her about Tony P was that he didn't get all grabby. The king size bed took up most of the room. He walked to one side of the bed, indicating she take the other, and together they folded back the covers. He climbed in and patted the empty space in the bed as she crawled across to join him. "Come here with yo' fine ass," he said with a grin as his mouth found hers in the dimly lit room and he pulled her close.

His mouth, hands and fingers worked methodically to ensure her readiness for him and he only whispered her name before he joined their bodies. Tony's movements were well placed and perfectly timed as he worked her body to a fevered pitch, bringing pleasure to her like she had never experienced. Her short nails raked across his back as his pace increased. Her body was covered in a fine patina of sweat as she moved with him, her eyes rolling upwards, her jaw slack, her breathing laborious. At one point, she tapped his shoulder to slow him down, because she had started to drool out the right side of her mouth like she'd had a stroke.

Tony pulled at her hair as he planted kisses along her neck, slowing his movements. "Jennifer, talk to me. Let me know you are enjoying our time together...."

She wanted to tell him it was good. In her mind, she was yelling from the rooftop how deep he was going and how fantastic she was feeling. Jennifer wanted to let him know she was climbing the summit and ready to explode, but instead, all she managed to utter was, "Nom... nom... nom...." And then more drool ran down her jaw.

In her ear, he told her she was holding back, and he needed her to let go. *Shit, I'm already drooling. If I let go anymore, it will not be cute.*

"Jen," he whispered as he increased his pace. His movements becoming more aggressive, rougher, filled with intensity.

His mouth found hers again as he kissed her deeply, making love to both her mouth and her body. "Tell me how I feel inside of you Jen..." he commanded her, but her words were lost in the sensations of his powerful movements. She tugged at his hair as she became aggressive with her tongue in his mouth and sent her hips into overdrive, matching his pace. He could feel her building, but Tony was about to lose it.

"I can't wait much longer, Jen," he said through gritted teeth as his movements became forceful. Each movement lifted her hips from the bed as he planted himself deeper each time. Her head flung back into the pillows and she cried out, her hips pushing upwards, trying to take in everything he was giving her. Tony matched her pace, calling her name with primal possession and he emptied his passion into her.

His fingers trailed across her face, feeling the smoothness of her bronze skin. "Wow, you are amazing," he said into her neck, planting a small kiss, then disengaging himself to go to the bathroom. Her body was buzzing from Tony's lovemaking. She was going to be really sore, but boy was she satisfied. She was uncertain if she should curl into a ball and suck her thumb or grab her panties and run home.

He called her from the other room. "All I need is seven minutes."

"Seven minutes for what?" She was almost afraid to ask.

"To reload for round two," he told her as he stood beside the bed, looking down at her with a wicked grin on his face.

She tried to sit up, but her muscles seemed to have failed everywhere but her neck, as she managed to lift her head, "What are you a rabbit?"

He started tamping the floor with his foot and shaking his thigh muscle. "Just call me Thumper!"

"Oh, dear Lord," she exclaimed as she tried to roll away, exposing her backside to him as Tony slid onto the bed and gathered her in his arms, flipping her to her back while kissing her breast and her belly. Seven minutes to the second he was ready for round two. Jennifer knew it was her fault just as he said, "You wound me up; I just have to burn it off."

Somewhere in the wee hours of the morning, when the energized rabbit fell into a deep slumber, Jennifer collected her things and let herself out. Unable to see in the dim light of the room and because she was feeling cross-eyed after their third round, she missed some of the spilled contents of her purse which had slid across the floor. Under the chair was still her driver's license, credit card and a few business cards.

If this was the caviar round, it was definitely an aperitif. Tony had ventured into a delightful cottage of hidden treats and he was eager to see where it would lead. Although Jennifer believed it would be a one-night stand and she had had gotten away clean, as the fairy tale goes, Gretel had inadvertently left a trail of blini for her handsome Hansel to come and find her.

A cold appetizer...

The Pretentious Puss was a small bistro that held about 20 tables. Jennifer's original idea of opening the eatery was to create a dining experience that was quaint with healthy food options. Thanks to her father and his big mouth, he was all the advertising she needed. In less than a week of opening, the lines were around the corner and Jennifer rarely got any time off. Her passion for something off the beaten path was now a commercial success and sucking the life out of what little life she led.

Never the type for one-night stands or casual relationships, the past year hadn't left her any time to do anything but cook and work. In her heart she wanted to start a family, but relationships weren't her forte. No matter how you sautéed, fried, or fricasseed it, love was an appetizer she preferred to serve cold. Her night with Tony was a hot and much needed distraction, but that is exactly what it was – a distraction. Today was Monday and she was back in the real world with solid reservations all week, a dinner party on Saturday night, and her old boss had called to ask her to cater a welcome party for a big pop singer who was coming to town. Yep. Busy. No time for a man or a family. Well, at least not this year.

Jennifer was happy about the warm afternoon. It was exceptionally warm, even in April in Atlanta. She needed to get out of the kitchen and take a break as she turned off the eyes of the cook stove to begin her moment of peace. Most of the prep for dinner service was complete, with the exception of preparing the leaves of romaine for the salads. The sous chef had lost the argument that whole leaf salads were much more expensive than purchasing the bags of mixed greens and it would increase their food costs. It was with patience that Jennifer explained that the whole leafs lasted longer and were fresher, giving the customers a better dining experience. The fresher experience increased the price by only a dime, which covered the cost and made a change for the little bistro that she was now struggling to love.

Love.

Ironic. Two nights ago, she told a random stranger that she loved him and then spent several hours making out with him as her pretend boyfriend followed by several hours in bed with him as a very real lover. She was still ridiculously sore from that adventure. The things that man did to her in bed had her reaching for imaginary clouds of orgasmic joy trying to hold on to her self-respect. Guilt wracked her brain for what she had done, as well as the idea of having a one-night stand. The sex had been so phenomenal that the guilt was being replaced by a slow creeping warmness that oozed through her body each time she thought about him.

He was funny. She had spent most of the night laughing and enjoying herself with him. Tony did have a wicked sense of humor. Well, the man was pretty wicked himself. *If only I had gotten his number.* Thoughts of her one night of abandon went out the window as she headed to the main floor to check the reservations for tonight. Mondays could be slow and if she could leave early tonight, that would be a plus. Just as she picked up the reservation book, the doorbell jangled.

"Deliveries are around back," she said without looking

up.

"Even for fresh flowers," the strong male voice said.

Jennifer's head popped up so fast her chef hat was slung from her head. *He's here! How did he find me?*

"Tony?"

In one hand he held a beautiful bouquet of wildflowers and in the other, her driver's license and credit card. "You dropped something," he told her as he handed her the cards. "I did give in to the urge to hit QVC and order a matching set of oven mitts with kittens on them."

Her mouth was still open, staring at him. In the daylight he was even sexier than in the soft light of night. In a pair of khakis and a red polo shirt, the man was making her lady parts salivate. Jennifer Taylor was at a loss for words. Unfortunately, Tony read her reaction the wrong way, and he was having trouble vocalizing his disappointment in her response to seeing him again. The one he was receiving was obviously not the one he expected.

"I'm sorry," he told her as he thrust the flowers at her. "I just thought I would return the cards... and... I am just going to find the nearest door and crawl under it. I am sorry to bother you."

He's walking away. Say something Jennifer. "Tony," she found her words. The man had a way of rendering her speechless, with or without her clothes on. "I'm sorry. I was just surprised to see you, that's all." She looked at the bouquet. "These are lovely. Let me see if I can find a vase or something to put these in. Have a seat."

When Jennifer returned to the main floor, Tony had taken a seat at a table for two by the window as he perused a menu. "Are you hungry, Tony?"

It took a concerted effort for his eyes not to rake her body. "I could stand a nibble or two."

"Great, how much time do you have?"

"I have all the time you need," he said with that same smile that had convinced her to take off her panties.

"Let me make you something," she told him as she pulled a chair up to the bar. "Come, sit. Do you like seafood?"

"Sure!"

"Any allergies I need to know about?"

"None," he said with almost too much excitement.

"Okay, we will start with a cold appetizer," she said as she seated her chef's hat back on her head and disappeared through the door to the kitchen. She came back a minute later with a shrimp cocktail. "That's my own special red sauce on those shrimp," she said as she scooped up the ice, dropped it into a glass, squeezed in some fresh lemon juice, added a shot of seltzer, and a splash of sweet & sour mix.

Tony could hear her in the kitchen and could smell the wonderful scents emitting from the back room. He wanted to watch her work. Hell, he wanted to pull her into his arms and kiss her again. For a second, his heart had dropped when she did not fling herself into his arms and confess her love for him. *What were you expecting? You played lover, dragged her to your room and ravished her until she escaped in the middle of the night.* In his mind, the way he saw it playing out was her feeling like Cinderella as he returned her means to buy more shoes. She had not missed either card or identification. Instead, he walked into coldness and her potential shame of what they had done two days ago. *But it felt so real.*

Jennifer brought out two salad plates, she placed one in front of him, the other at the spot next to him. "My extra special dressing. The recipe is secret," she winked at him and disappeared through the door again. Next time she returned with Prosciutto-wrapped asparagus, seared scallops and a perfectly portioned serving of brown rice. Or at least he thought it was brown until he tasted it. But before she even let him sink his fork into anything, she blessed the food. "Bon Appetit."

He tasted the rice and his eyes rolled up into his head. "What is this yummy deliciousness that is dancing in my mouth?"

Her brow was furrowed. "You do have a creative way with words don't you?"

He chuckled. "I'd better, considering it is what I do for a living."

Her eyes grazed him. "I would have thought you were a fitness model or personal trainer with that body."

"You make me blush. Um, thanks, I think," he smiled as he cut into the scallops. He was chewing and staring at her. "This is amazing."

His eyes got wide as he plopped another scallop into his mouth, and he was grinning like the Cheshire Cat. "You are perfect! This is perfect! Oh my goodness! This is just too perfect to be real!"

Jennifer stopped chewing. "What are you talking about?"

"You just may have saved my life," he told her as he hummed his way through the rest of lunch.

Tony Peay was a single father of an unusual 12-year-old with a refined palate. So refined that junk food, pizza and anything processed did not go into her mouth. He was partly to blame because he ate a rather natural and wholesome diet that sometimes bordered on bland. At the wonderful age of 8, Sasha, his little angel, began a small herb garden in the backyard and used the contents to season the foil wrapped fish her dad insisted upon serving every Friday night.

Fresh rosemary was harvested to go on the grill with the dry chicken breast he used to cook. As she aged, so did her adventure in the kitchen. Try as he may to keep up, he just was not able. Her growth in four years was astounding. His sister, Cleo, has been an angel with the care and assistance in raising Sasha, but last week, she threw in the towel. Two weeks before Sasha's 13th birthday party, Cleo refused to lend a hand.

"Tony, she is too spoiled. No one is going to spend that kind of money on food for a bunch of 12 and 13-year-old girls who can't even pronounce half of the stuff she wants to serve," Cleo said with firmness.

"There has to be a compromise, Cleo. Will you try to find one?" he pleaded with her.

"No. You and Mom can deal with this nonsense, but I, for one, am not serving buffalo mozzarella to a bunch of teenagers! It is indulgent, expensive and honestly, just ridiculous. She has too much control in your life, Tony. It has to stop," Cleo said as she picked up her things and walked out of the door.

In some instances, he knew his sister was right. Tony had not dated in years because he was always too concerned about his daughter's feelings. It was at his sister's insistence that he was even in the hotel on Saturday night. Cleo booked the room for him for the weekend and told him to go and get lucky. Friday night, he sat in the bar on that same stool nursing a similar drink only to be approached by several ladies that even in his lonely, horned up state, he wasn't willing to deal with. Just as he was about the wrap up the leftovers and head to his room to order a movie, Jennifer approached him with a lovely offer too good to refuse.

"Jennifer, I am a single dad of a 12-year-old with a sophisticated palate." He waited for her reaction and the million questions that normally followed that statement. Silly questions about his relationship with the child's mother. Insipid questions about whether or not he was still seeing her, or if they were they romantically involved. The kind of questions from women that supported his reasons to remain single.

This lady said nothing, but waited for the rest of his statement. He went on, "In two weeks she is celebrating her 13th birthday. I am throwing her a party with 15 to 20 of her braces wearing, acne prone little friends and she wants a specialized menu."

"Okay, what is your budget?" Jennifer asked.

Tony stared at her. He didn't really know what to say. Where were the rest of the crazed personal questions? "I guess about $500 on the high end," he said as he swallowed hard.

"If you want me to cater it, I will need to see your

kitchen so I can determine how much I prepare on site and the set up space. I will also need to meet with your daughter to see what we can come up with that fits your budget and her vision," she said as rose to go to the kitchen to get a slice of cheesecake and some coffee for them both. "I drink decaf, what about you?"

"No coffee for me. I am a tea drinker," he said, still in a bit of shock.

"Herbal or decaf tea?" she called from the kitchen.

"Herbal," he said as she returned with a box for him to make a selection and a mini pot of hot water.

She placed a piece of paper in front of him. "I am off on Wednesday. I can stop by your house then and meet with her. Write your address and number here."

He complied with the request, but he was so floored, he pulled her into his arms, his mouth against her ear, and said, "Jennifer, I love you."

Her breath caught in her throat, but she would not buy into it. "That was almost as good as mine on Saturday night. I think I was more convincing, though," she said as she looked into his eyes. Her fingers came up to his lips, running tentatively across the bottom lip and down his neck. "No, Tony. I love you."

She twisted her mouth a little to the right, making a wiseguy impression. "See, if you're gonna do it, it has to be said with feeling."

"I guess I will have to practice a bit more," he said as he looked at her. *She is an amazing woman.*

"You do that," she told him as she took a business card from the bar and wrote her cell phone number on the back. "Now get out. I have a dinner service to set up."

"Jen," he said softly.

She answered without looking up as she stacked their dirty dish plates. "Yeah, Tony, what's up?"

"May I kiss you again before I leave?"

"Hell no! The last time you started kissing me that led to something else, which left me walking sideways all day yesterday. You need to take your ass on home or somewhere else," she told him as she collected the dirty cups, mumbling to herself.

He rushed to her side. "Jennifer, I'm sorry. Did I hurt you?"

"Yes, you did," she told him with a look of incredulity on her face. It was the twinkle in her eye that prompted his next question.

"But did you like it?"

"Yes, I did. Now get out, before I start wanting seconds," she said with a grin.

That was all he needed. His hand went to her cheek. "Anytime... anyplace... any moment of the day or night, I will be yours," he told her as her heartbeat increased. He planted a feathery kiss on her lips with just a tad bit of tongue and he left.

"Well, shoot!" Jennifer said as she went into the kitchen and went back to work. Tony, on the other hand, was reeling with thoughts and ideas. At times, he wished he had a brother in which to talk things over with, share stories or even adventures. *Yes. Having a brother would be nice, then I could tell him all about Jennifer.*

Tino Boehner was thinking the same thing. It would

be nice to sit and have a conversation with his brother. Now that he was aware that he had one in Tony, he really wanted to get to know him. Right now, he sat at the kitchen table with his new girlfriend Ebony Miller wondering how in the world he was going to pull this off. How do you show up on your mother's doorstep and yell, "Hey Mom, I'm home?" Especially after she gave you away to be raised by someone else.

At 30 years old, Valentino Boehner was a self-made man and one of the best real estate gurus in the greater Raleigh area, but he knew something was missing inside of him. He was shocked when he asked his adoptive parents about his birth mother, only to find that he knew her. She had remained a part of his life and showed up at all of his major life events. The only issue was that for the majority of his life, his birth mother masqueraded as his cousin.

He looked at his graduation picture from college. She stood beside him with a smile and the young man he also called cousin, Tony. Ebony sat next to Tino on the couch and rubbed his thigh. "I think – and this is just me talking – that if you want to get to know your birth family, start with him." She pointed at the boy in the picture.

"You think I should start with Tony?"

"I would. He is your brother after all, and maybe," she paused for a minute, "I dunno, maybe if you get to know him first, it may be easier to understand why she kept him and not you. You know, see how he was raised."

Tino gave it some thought. His mother also said that there was a girl. "I also have a sister, based on what my mother said." His eyes glazed over as he stared at the photo he had been holding for nearly a month.

"Well, if you want answers, we start with your brother. Which one of you is older?"

"He is. I think. By two years," Tino said.

Ebony looked over his shoulder at the photo, "You think he has any kids? His kids would also have an uncle now. Wouldn't that be cool?"

Tino only smiled at her a bit as he looked at the photo again. It would be cool to get to know his brother. There were some properties he was interested in seeing in Atlanta, as well. Maybe he would schedule a trip to meet his family.

A thick soup...

Change can come slowly, subtly, and ease its way into your life like an addiction to fried foods. At first it is the crunch of that chicken skin that gets you, then the salt, and before you know it, it's two in the morning and you are riding through town looking for an all-night KFC. Kids have the same effect on women. Tony's daughter was very similar to her father, subtle, yet a force that worked its way into your life and lodged in your throat like a sideways chicken bone.

The first thing Jennifer noticed about Sasha Peay was that she was very protective of her father. The second thing Jennifer understood was that the girl had her father wrapped around her finger. This resonated loud and clear, because women had said the same thing about her after her mother passed.

Women can be like vultures. One body may not even be completely dead before they start to come in and pick at what remains. Her mother was battling cancer in the upstairs back room of their home while well-wishing women were in the front of the house making a play for her husband. Jennifer's sister, Gloria, who was older by two years, considered herself to be a devout lesbian, full of anger and resentment, who made it clear to any of the women, that if they moved into the home, they would have to contend with her first. The second point of contention was Jennifer. If she didn't like you or want you around her father, then the front door was the way you needed to go. Unlike Gloria, who had the spirit and demeanor of their mother, Jennifer was an easygoing soul like her father.

Well, he used to be until he retired and had nothing to do all day. The sadness in his daily phone calls to her was what prompted Jennifer to leave her job in Los Angeles and return home to Atlanta – a cushy job as a personal chef to one of the biggest talent agents in the Hollywood game. If you wanted it, Laney Myers was the person who got it for you. She was heartbroken when Jennifer left, but she understood. Family is everything. She also knew that Jennifer's dad was everything to her as well. Moreover, Jen missed the old fart.

Or at least she thought she did until she moved back home. Being around your dad as a young girl, you see your daddy with stars in your eyes. Your dad can do no wrong. Being around your father as a grown woman, Jennifer began to believe that he gave her mother cancer. Her mother accepted it as a means of escape from Johnny Taylor, who could worry the stank off a poop pile. Right now, he was a proverbial albatross around her childless neck that was dead, reeking and worrying the shit out her. After meeting with Sasha Peay, she was beginning to think maybe her dad and this little girl would be perfect companions to each other.

Sasha opened the door when Jennifer rang the bell. She was cute as a button with dark brown hair, large expressive eyes and braces that were brightly colored in a rainbow of hues. What struck Jennifer immediately was the muscle tone of the child. *Gymnast?* She thought as she walked past the girl into the front room of the house. The home was located in Brookwood Hills off of Brighton

Road. It was a modern home with lots of windows and plenty of natural light.

"You must be Sasha? I'm Jennifer Taylor, your chef for your 13th birthday party." That kind of an introduction immediately put her in good standing with the child, who welcomed her into the home amid a flurry of ideas. Ideas that started with where she wanted the food displayed. "I'm thinking we can move the dining room table out and maybe use a couple of eight-foot tables to set up the food," she told Jennifer.

"I am Sasha Peay," she said as if it were an afterthought. To the empty space that fed into the living room, she yelled, "Hey, Dad. The chef is here. Can we take out this good rug so no food is spilled on it?" She showed Jennifer the galley kitchen, never missing a beat. "There is plenty of room in the fridge for storage of cold items like the sushi, and of course, we have a double oven for the warm foods and appetizers that will be served."

Jennifer asked, "Do you have a theme for your party?"

Sasha stopped mid step. "I haven't thought about that. A theme?" she asked as she stared up at the ceiling.

"Let's sit down first, discuss your budget, a party concept and then take a look at where we can go from there," Jennifer said as she pointed at the kitchen table. Tony said nothing as she walked by him, briefly shaking his hand and acknowledging he was actually in the room. She pointed at a chair for him to join them at the table. From her satchel, she took out two notepads and two calculators, passing one of each to Sasha.

"From what your father told me, you have a budget of $500, which doesn't include my fee. You are also expecting 15-20 of your friends so sushi for that many people, even if you were serving California rolls, is labor intensive and will eat up $300 right off the top of your budget." She watched Sasha's face drop.

"But I have an idea," she told the girl with a smile. "You seem to be health conscious and physically fit. How about a Wii Fit party?"

Sasha looked confused. "I'm not understanding."

"Some teen girls do makeover or makeup parties. I was thinking since you are health conscious, you could do something different, with like maybe a Wii Fit yoga session, a bowling tournament or even a tennis match with some group dance," Jennifer said and noticed Tony smiling. "That way, your menu can be cost effective by having a smoothie bar, crudités and healthy food choices without shoving your healthy lifestyle choice down your friends' throats."

The girl sat quietly for a minute. She tapped the pen against her cheek, squinted her eyes and said, "If I go with this option, can we work in some buffalo mozzarella?"

"If I do it as a small appetizer on beefsteak tomatoes with fresh basil, then we can get away with about $30 worth," Jennifer replied.

The girl was cheery. "I have tons of fresh basil growing in the backyard, so you won't have to buy any of that."

"My next question, Ms. Peay. Are any of your friends staying over?"

"Yes, at least seven will spend the night," she said as she looked at her dad.

Jennifer began to scribble down some notes on the pad, made some calculations and started calling out food, figures and facts to Sasha, who scribbled away on the paper. "Your total now, Ms. Peay?"

"$375!"

"Great," Jennifer told her. "What you must factor in as well is some sort of starch. I would suggest we do a grits station."

"A what? Grits? Like in for breakfast?" Her face was scrunched up in distaste.

"Hear me out," Jennifer said as she explained the idea. The grits would serve as a base to add in cheese, Andouille sausage, shrimp, mushrooms and scrambled eggs. "This way, any leftovers will be perfect for breakfast the next morning." She called out a few more numbers. "Your total now, Ms. Peay?"

"$487! Dad. We did it! I'm bringing it all in under budget!" She ran around the table and flung her body at Jennifer, throwing her arms around her neck and placing a sloppy kiss on her cheek. "OMG I love you! You're the best!" She asked to be excused and her voice could be heard down the hall on her phone with her BFF Emily as she bragged about the cool chef her dad had hired for her party. "It is going to be a Wii Fit party, so we need to coordinate our games, okay, Em?"

It was a thick soup, but it seemed easy to swallow. She made a few notes on her tablet and collected the extra calculator, leaving the pad on the table.

"You are amazing. Do you know that?" Tony asked her.

She scoffed at him. "Of course I know that. And now, so do you." She grinned at him.

"I already knew it. This... this just confirms it. The way you handled her, brought her into the process, made her a part of it. I just... I don't... wow," he said with wide eyes.

"Don't get too happy, yet. You don't know my rates."

He stopped grinning. "What are we talking here, 100 bucks an hour?"

"More like 500. But you... I may let you work it off, with yo' fine ass," she said with a chuckle.

He lowered his voice but did not move from where he stood. "Again, Jennifer, anytime... any place... any moment of the day or night, I will be yours," he said with a mischievous grin.

"Good Lawd!" she said as she crossed her legs, wiggled her hips and collected her things. "I'll send you an invoice so I can start buying the items."

She shook his hand again and made her exit.

6

A thin soup...

"Chef Jennifer," she said into the cell phone as she tried to sort through the wrong shipment of cabbage that came from the market.

"Jen, it's Tony," he responded. She could hear the tension in his voice.

"What's up?"

"I have a couple of problems. The date Sasha booked her party is the same night of the Kitty Berry concert and her friends are all going. She is pretty upset," he said in the line.

"Does she have an alternate date in mind?"

Tony sighed heavily. "That's why I called. Is it an inconvenience for you to stop by tonight?"

"Yes," she said tersely.

Tony was unclear about what she was saying. "Yes, you can stop by or yes, it is an inconvenience."

"It is an inconvenience and no, I can't stop by. I will have my assistant print my schedule and you two come by here tonight. I will make you dinner," she said. "Will that work?"

He was surprised at how smoothly she transitioned everything. "Yes, we can do that."

"See you at about six," and she hung up the phone.

Tony was feeling a bit off key because of the conversation earlier with Jennifer. She had been almost rude to him on the phone, but maybe he was reading too much into it. He dressed for the evening, trying to make sure he looked good. Why, he was uncertain. He and Sasha had added a bit of color to their wardrobe as she wore a brightly colored yellow dress and he a matching yellow tie. He was stressing a bit because she told him to be at the restaurant at six yet it took him nearly 20 minutes to find a parking space.

Once inside, he found out why. There was at least a 30-minute wait for a table, the quaint little bistro he had lunch in a few days ago was now a madhouse full of customers. A young man dressed in all black asked, "Do you have a reservation?"

"Ah, Chef Taylor is expecting us," Tony said with some hesitation.

"Mr. Peay and Sasha?"

"Yes," Tony said.

"Follow me," the waiter told them as he led them through the throng of tables, past the bar, into a private area near the back. "Can I take your drink order?"

Sasha ordered a lemonade and Tony an unsweetened ice tea as they waited for either Jennifer or a menu to arrive. Five minutes later, she came out of the back with a chef's rag on her head, two salads and a blank look on her face. "Hey guys," she said as she took a seat.

"Wow, you guys are really busy," Tony told her as he looked about.

"No, this is about normal for a Thursday. Friday and Saturday nights are the money makers and speaking of which," she said as she turned in the chair and raised her hand. A pretty young blonde in an apron came over with several sheets of loose paper. She gave Tony a huge grin and he returned a smile, yet his eyes were on Jennifer, who paid neither of them any real attention.

"Chastity, please go ahead and bring out the dinner for these two, while I go over some new numbers," she told the server, who grinned at Tony again before she bounded off.

To Sasha, Jennifer asked, "So what is the new date you have in mind?"

The girl sampled the dressing. "This is really good. Did you make this, Chef Jennifer?" She poured the vinaigrette over her salad. "It's yummy. Oh, sorry, I was thinking the following Saturday."

Jennifer thumbed through the stack of papers and located the date. "So you are looking at two days of prep work, plus pulling me off an extremely busy and profitable night. Hmm," she looked at the girl. "Let me see your hands, Sasha?" She showed Jennifer her hands. "How good are your knife cuts?"

Sasha crinkled her brow. "What do you mean knife cuts?"

Jennifer stood up and went to the kitchen, returning moments later with a zucchini and a paring knife, along with a mini cutting board. "Show me how you would cut this vegetable." She also had Tony's attention, who watched his daughter snip the ends, and make a clean slice down the middle. Carefully and meticulously, she cut even sizes of the vegetable and laid it on the tray. Sasha was very proud of her work. Secretly so was Jennifer, but she had a couple of surprises for the young lady as she praised her work.

"In order for me to make your next date, you are going to have to come and work here at my side to learn to prep the food for your party."

Sasha's mouth got wide. "Why? I mean my dad can pay you for your time. Why do I have to come and work here?" She said the last part as if *here* was the soup kitchen down on Peachtree.

Jennifer pulled a zucchini out her pocket and laid it on the cutting board. From her chef's coat sleeve, she removed her favorite paring knife. In two flicks of her wrist, she snipped both ends of the squash, made four even slices and her wrist skimmed so fast that the vegetable was laid out with a decorative design and in perfectly even sizes. "Because my time is valuable. Your father told you there was a budget. You cannot just assume that the money in his account is there for you to use for whatever you need. If you want me to cater your party, you are going to have to help me get everything ready for it."

Sasha looked at her father who said nothing. He wasn't sure what Jennifer was doing, but he would go along with it for now. "Dad, can't you just pay her?"

He had to ask. "Chef Taylor, how much will it cost me for changing the date?"

"It will cost you $5,000. Or you can go with another chef," she told Tony with a flat expression.

Tony took the cue. "So what time will Sasha need to be here and on what dates?"

Sasha was visibly upset until Jennifer spoke to her softly. "Sweetheart, you cannot believe that your father will be able to buy or write a check for everything you want. Some things, you must work to have. And other times, life will give you a very thin bowl of soup that you have to be willing to add some things in order to make it palatable. This is my business. I cannot leave my business and shut down my ability to make a living to come and cook for your birthday. I am willing to be there for you, but you have to be willing to be there for me, as well. Can you do that?"

"Yes, I guess so," she said as their dinners arrived.

"Good, I have to get back to work. Enjoy your dinners. Bon Appetit."

Tony was starting to like Jennifer Taylor more and more.

"Dad," Sasha touched his arm while he was driving. "Is it true what she said?"

Tony kept his eyes on the road. "What do you mean, sweetie? Is what true?" Although he knew what she was referring to, he wanted to give her an opportunity to vocalize what was on her mind.

"About you not being able to write a check for everything I need? I mean, we are rich, right?"

Tony started to choke. "No, we are not. By no means, whatsoever. We are better off now that we were a few years ago, when it took everything I had to keep the lights on and pay the mortgage. But, we are a long way from rich, darling."

"So, how did Chef Jennifer know that we didn't have enough money to change the date and pay her?"

He thought about it as he maneuvered his 6-year-old

car through the nighttime Atlanta traffic. "Because your budget for this party is what she gets paid an hour."

Sasha's mouth dropped. "She is paid $500 per hour?"

"Yes, she is," he told her.

She stared out the window quietly. "So how did you manage to get her to do this for me?"

"She owed me a favor," he said softly as he thought about the feel of Jennifer under him, how responsive she was to his touch. In truth, he was more in her debt than anything. One night with her and he felt more alive than he had in years.

"I will do a good job and make you proud, Daddy, and I will learn everything she can teach me about cooking," she said as they pulled up in front of their home.

"Fair enough," he said as she kissed his cheek and went to her room. Jennifer had made a very clear point to them both and he felt like an idiot. His daughter had no understanding of money, time, or anything other than what he gave her. All of the time Cleo had been telling him the same thing, and one conversation with Sasha, Jennifer had broken through.

Even if he added some chunks to the pot, he was still swimming in a thin soup with no nourishment. He looked upwards and pressed his hands together. "Lord, order my steps...."

His train of thought was broken by the ringing of his landline. *Who can that be?* Tony yelled down the hall to Sasha that he had picked up the call.

"Hello," he said into the receiver.

"Tony, this is Tino Boehner."

It took him a minute to remember the cousin his mother often dragged him off to see. "Oh, hey, cuz, what's going on?"

"I was heading to the ATL in a few weeks and was wondering if we could get together for dinner, maybe a drink or something?"

Tony saw no problem with it. "Sure, let me give you my cell, and let me know, I would love to see you. I'm sure Mom would as well."

It was so sudden, so abrupt that Tony was taken aback. "No," Tino said, "I don't want to see your mother on this visit. Just us guys. I will see her on another trip."

"Okay," Tony said as they worked out the details and he hung up. He dismissed the abruptness as thoughts of Jennifer filled his head.

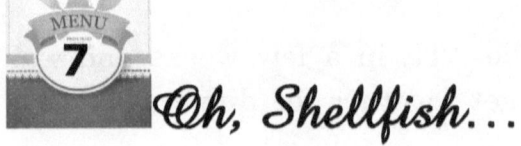

Oh, Shellfish...

We never walk through life alone. Even in your darkest hours and brightest moments, there is someone at your side to either regale your achievements or laugh at your failures. Yet, some are lucky to find friendship that crosses the line into family and brotherhood. Raheem Bonner was that type of friend to Tony Peay.

Right now, he sat on the couch, pretending to watch whatever dumb movie his best friend of 23 years had ordered from Netflix. He found it more interesting to watch Tony, who obviously wasn't watching the movie either. He knew he wasn't watching the movie because he was sitting there, staring at the ceiling with a really dumb look on his face. Tony almost appeared happy. Normally, when and if he landed a lucrative contract for a graphic design project, he would have this look. But the twinkle in his eyes suggested Tony P had scored some one-on-one game time with a lady.

"Dude, you are sitting there like you just ripped a bean burrito fart that had been lodged in your lower intestines all day," he said to Tony, who turned and looked at him with a face full of concern.

"For you to be a writer, your analogies and similes are rather disturbing and very base considering your overly expensive education," Tony told him.

"Come on, spill it."

"Spill what, Raheem?"

"Who is she and what does she do?"

The grin that covered his friend's face lit up the entire

room. "I don't know what to tell you. I mean, I guess, we are kind of seeing each other," Tony exhaled. "I really like her and oh man, how she deals with Sasha is amazing."

Raheem sat up on the couch. "Stop. Wait. Hold it right there! She's met Sasha already?"

"Yeah, and Sasha likes her. Well she did until Jen told her she had to come and do some work for this birthday party thing," he was laughing. "The look on Sasha's face was priceless!"

Raheem's jaw was hanging loosely as he gawked at Tony. "Hold the hell up! Back up and tell me everything. Where did you meet... wait, when did you meet her?"

"I met her last Saturday and..."

"... Last Saturday and she has met your daughter?"

"Yeah, it was funny actually. Jen picked me up in the hotel bar at the Marriott," he said as he started to laugh.

"No. It's not funny. Some woman in a bar picked you up and you've introduced her to your daughter already? After only a week?"

To say that Tony P was smiling would be to trivialize the expression on his face. The look he held was more like a diabetic standing in front of the display case in an Amish bakery. The loopy distant gaze. The semi-smile smirk. The forward thrust chin and eyebrows that had slid down the sides of his forehead, giving him a puppy-like appearance. Raheem reached over and punched him.

"Snap out of it!"

"No! And you can't make me!" Tony told him as he stuck out his tongue.

"Back up and start from the top," Raheem demanded. Tony was all too happy to oblige. For the next 30 minutes, he filled him in on the meeting in the bar, the class reunion, his invitation to his room, which made him grabbed a pillow to cover his lap just thinking about it. He told his longtime friend about the credit card, the flowers, feeling like an intruding fool and her making him a light lunch. "She is an amazing chef," he said with pride.

"That's how she came to meet Sasha," he told Raheem.

It did not escape Raheem's notice. "Out of curiosity, Tony, did it ever occur to you that maybe Cleo was right? That Sasha is too spoiled and is accustomed to getting everything she wants from you?"

"I know, right? And that is what I mean about Jen handling her so well," he said again with even more pride.

Tony went on to explain about Jennifer coming to the house and the initial meeting keeping Sasha on budget. He spoke to Raheem about the change of dates and then, he stood up as he attempted to demonstrate how proficient Jennifer had been with the knife. He was in full on roleplaying as he described Sasha's voice and facial expression. "Man, you should have seen it. She handled her so well, and when she got to the thin soup analogy, I knew. I knew!"

"You knew what?" Raheem's eyebrows were up.

"I want something more with her," he said as he flopped down on the couch. "I really like this woman, Raheem. I like her a lot."

"What do you know about her other than where she works and what she does for a living?"

"I... uh..." Tony stopped. That was all he knew. That, where she went to high school and the year she graduated. Based on the school and the zoning, he had a general idea of where she grew up.

Raheem felt like a defense attorney. "I rest my case."

"Oh, shellfish!" Tony said. Raheem was right. He was jumping the gun and had a great deal more to learn about the lady chef. He changed the subject. "Hey, I got a call from my cousin, Tino, the other day.

Raheem didn't move. "He said he was coming to town and wanted to get together, you know, guy stuff. I don't know what to do with him. What is guy stuff?"

Slowly, turning to face Tony, Raheem said, "Your cousin?"

"Yeah, I told you about him. Tino Boehner. We went to his high school and college graduation in North Carolina."

"Your cousin, Tino, from North Carolina?"

Tony was getting irritated. "What are you, a parrot? That's what I said."

"Like that real estate dude, Tino Boehner?"

"Yeah, that's him," Tony said, surprised. "You heard of him?"

"Everybody has heard of him, you idiot! No kidding, that is your cousin? I want to meet him... I want to meet this chef, too," Raheem said.

Tony was quiet as he tried to figure out how to broach the subject of Jennifer's race, not that it should matter. He sighed. Then waited. He sighed again. Then waited.

"Oh, for the love of football, man, spit it out," Raheem yelled at him.

"No, I was trying to work something out in my head. You know when he comes to town, maybe we can go out as a group, on a date or something, if he brings his wife... girlfriend or whatever...."

He looked at Raheem. Maybe now was not the time to tell him Jennifer was black.

"Yeah, I will rustle up one of my ladies to come with...."

Tony left it at that, saying no more.

Antipasto...

At 11:30, Tony sat behind his computer, staring at the latest renderings of a vector for an album cover for a local hip hop record label. It had been years since he worked with the owner on a new album release, and it felt good to work this side of his brain. Most of the work he did as a graphic design artist were small jobs for independent authors, small businesses and one-offs from ad agencies. It was lucrative enough to keep the mortgage paid and the power on. He was a fast and clean designer who normally got the concept right the first time, which also saved time, billable hours and increased his chances for bonuses. Rarely, if ever, did he take on a project that would last more than a month. Last year, he landed a contract with a small architectural firm that put him way over in the black. He loved his job and being able to work from home.

It had been a necessity initially as a single father. The cost of day care was ridiculous, he was in college, and had to move back home with his mother and sister. It had all been worth it in the end. He still managed to finish college on time, studying, working a part-time job to keep Sasha in diapers and formula, and to maintain some balance in his life. It was an early lesson in love that made him move away from trying to date, when he broke up with a young lady whom Sasha had become attached to when she was two years old. After that mistake, he swore the only woman that would meet his daughter would be the one he planned to marry.

I am not sure what Jen means or how any of this is going to pan out ... but I am going to see this one through.

Tony picked up his phone and dialed her number.

"Chef Taylor, how may I help you," her soft voice spoke into the phone.

"I was just thinking about you. I thought I would call," he found himself holding his breath.

"That's nice of you. What are you up to?" Jennifer asked as she sat on the side of the bed.

"I'm feeling some kind of way. Out of sorts I guess," he told her with some apprehension.

Jennifer picked up on it immediately. "I know what you mean. I met you a week ago, by accident, and now I am in the inner sanctum, about to get into some serious fruit and vegetable cutting with your daughter." She kicked off her shoes so she could lay back on the bed. "Who is as cute as a button I might add."

It was quiet on the other end of the line as he released the air he was holding in his lungs. "Thank you. She is a bit precocious, but she's mine." The air was thick with unsaid verses as he swam through the seconds, trying to get to the next minute of lined up words. "I like you, Jen. I like you a lot."

"You are pretty cool yourself there, Tony P."

"I would like to know more about you," he said as he shut down his computer.

"Me? There isn't much to tell. I cook for a living, which is how I feed and clothe myself. Being good at what I do leaves me little time to do anything else. That's my life in an antipasto dish," she told him.

"What about relationships, a love life, a past love," he was curious to know.

"I am divorced. My love life for the past two years has consisted of me getting lucky a week ago with a stranger in his hotel room."

It was the last thing he was expecting to hear from her, but the cat was out of the bag and he wanted to know more. "Any children?"

"Much to father's chagrin, no," was all she gave.

Tony was more interested now than before. "You don't give away much do you?"

"I just..." She stopped talking.

"Say what's on your mind. We should be able to do that with each other. Tell me what you need. Tell me what you want. Tell me you want me," he said softly.

"I would like to spend more time with you, Tony. But I don't know what this is. I don't know what I'm doing with any of this. I don't know what I am doing with you... us... and then there is Sasha," the concern was emanating from her voice. She had been introduced to his daughter. In the next week she was going to make a definite impression in her life. *What if it went south?*

"Whatever this is, I like it. And I want more," he told her with a firm voice.

I don't understand any of this. What is he up to? What does Tony want from me? Instead of having a one-sided conversation in her head, she spoke it aloud. "What do you want from me, Tony?"

Failure to be honest with his feelings and emotions had left him in a cycle of doubt and uncertainty about his future. In a few years, his daughter would be off having fun and enjoying her life and he would still be on the couch with Raheem watching B-Flicks on demand. The past 12 years had been dedicated to being a great father to his daughter, but Jennifer was new life. He felt as if he had a chance to rejoin the human race. To love. To give love. To be honest. "Jen, I want to get a point when the next time you look in my eyes and say *Tony, I love you*, it's for real."

There it was.

In the open.

In the air and floating.

"Fair enough, Tony. Good night," she said.

"Good night, Jen."

"My marriage didn't work because I had the wrong expectations," she told Tony over the phone the next day. It was a quiet Sunday afternoon. Her father was snoring loudly on the couch, waking up sporadically, yelling, "Don't change my channel!" She wasn't paying much attention to the spaghetti western, which was cliché with bandits, men throwing bullets from unloaded weapons and the sound effects completed by an editor who must have fallen asleep at the helm. The gun would fire and 5 seconds later, the sound would come. *Gotta love my dad.*

Her dad was her first real love. Johnny Taylor had set the standard of how a man should treat his princess, but he never warned her about the men who would manipulate her love as her husband Michael had.

"I have only been back from Los Angeles for 18 months. I am living back home with my dad who retired last year," she said.

In LA, she was the personal chef to a big time Hollywood agent. A power player in the game with the big dogs. Jennifer loved her job and she was phenomenal at cooking meals and catering special events for small clients to premier red carpet events. It was also where she met Michael.

"He was everything a girl could want. Tall, good looking, broad shoulders and a smile that would melt chocolate on a cold day," she confessed. Initially, she met him at a small function. He came as someone's plus one. "I was putting more antipasto out, with beautiful olives and bruschetta, when he walked up to me and started a conversation about my food. I was flattered."

The flattery didn't stop there. Unbeknownst to Jennifer, Michael knew exactly who she was and who she worked for, and it was his way in. "We went on a few dates, then it got really serious really fast. We ran off to Vegas, got hitched and suddenly I was married to an up-and-coming actor," she blew into the phone.

"An up-and-comer who decided to help me out at one of my boss's larger functions," she said with some melancholy. "He worked the room like a champ."

In less than six months of marriage, he managed to score some walk-on roles and several TV gigs with lines. "By the 9-month period, he somehow managed to get my boss to get him a role in a major Hollywood blockbuster, with more than one line. It went from there," Jennifer said into the line.

Tony listened to her words and could hear the pain in her voice. "So you are saying he used you?"

"Used is a small word for what he did. What he did was a betrayal. He married me to get to my boss. A boss who would do anything for me, and a woman who thought that getting my husband a leg up in the business was her way of giving back to me," Jennifer said. "I didn't know and didn't understand. I was naïve."

Her naiveté was short lived when she came home to find him running lines with a costar. The next time he was practicing a lovemaking scene. The time after that he was actually method acting with the love-making passage. "Then he started to make the Hollywood scene. I was catering the red carpet events while he was walking it."

"I was proud of him, Tony. He was living his dream, then he got a larger role, which took him on location overseas," she said with far too much pain in her voice.

"That's when all the pictures started to surface," she said. "Of course he told me it was all publicity and press, but I knew better."

It only worsened the situation when her boss pulled her to the side and told her, "Guys like Michael are a dime a dozen. He will have a few more big movies and he will crash and burn. His type always does. Get out while you can."

"I listened. I filed for divorce after the release of the movie and took half of his assets. When it all cleared, I cashed the check and moved back home. It is how I opened the bistro," she said.

"It's so cool that you own your own restaurant," he added, uncertain why he was feeling a sense of pride in her accomplishment.

"Yes. But being the boss doesn't give me a lot of time off. I am closed on Sundays and off on Wednesdays, and every other Saturday," she replied.

"I can work with that," he told her.

Jennifer was smiling, even after her father woke up, passed gas, looked around like someone else had done it, and went back to sleep. Jen got up from the couch and went to the kitchen. "I'm not damaged, Tony. I'm wary."

"You? Hell, I am scared out of my mind. I mean for the past two days, my daughter has been mutilating vegetables trying to make roses out of radishes. I have no idea what she did to that honeydew and she is constantly trying to *get it right*, so she can impress you," he told her with a tinge of anger in his voice. "If this goes wrong..."

"If it does not go between us, I will handle her with respect and as her own person."

"You would do that?"

"Yes. She is a child and should not be in the middle of adult issues. Besides, I like her. She is a cool kid," Jennifer said to him. "What about you?" She left it open-ended.

"What about me?" He knew this was where she was going to ask the questions about Sasha's mother.

Jennifer asked, "Any brothers and sisters?"

He didn't know why, but he felt disappointed that she didn't seem to want to know about that part of his life. "I have a sister, her name is Cleopatra. We call her Cleo."

"Wow, what is up with that? Your mom must be a big movie buff?"

Tony was confused. "Yes, she is. Why do you say that?"

"Anthony and Cleopatra? Are you two twins?"

He laughed because until now, he had never made the connection between their names. "No, we are not. I am older by four years. What about you? Any siblings?"

Jennifer exhaled loudly. "I have a sister, who is also the bane of my father's existence. She has the personality of my mother but looks like my daddy."

"So I take it you look like your mother?"

"Yes, but I have my dad's personality... thank God for small favors."

His curiosity was piqued, and he found himself smiling. "Why is that?"

She searched for the right words. "Have you ever seen someone so ugly that they are kind of cute?"

"No. No, I have not," he said flatly.

"Well, that's my sister," she said very solemnly.

"Must have been tough growing up with you being so statuesque and drop dead gorgeous," he said.

Jennifer was getting warm from her toes all the way up to her... "Well, you are just saying that to get in my pants again."

"I am saying it because I mean it, and we both know I am getting in your pants again. Several more times, in fact. Hell, if I had my way, I would wake up with your pants on my head." He was laughing.

The line was quiet. "Jen," he said.

"Yes, Tony?"

"Did you enjoy making love to me as much as I did you?"

Her breath was uneven, the room was hot and so was she. "Yes, I did."

His last words stayed with her for a minute, even after he hung up. "Jen, anytime ... any place ... any moment of the day or night, I will be yours. You have but to give me the command."

"Command? Aren't we melodramatic?"

"No, I am telling you what I want and what I need," he said firmly.

"What is it you need, Tony P?"

"I need to be yours," he said and bid her goodnight.

That's a lot of pasta...

Sometimes, what you want and what you need can be diametrically opposed to what must occur for a life to move forward. What Tony P wanted was to see Jennifer. The thing he needed was to be back in her arms, feeling her lips on him, her hands roaming his body as she surrendered to her passion. Most of all, he wanted her to want him. All of these cravings in the middle of the night prompted a surprise visit to her little bistro on Tuesday afternoon.

"I am in the neighborhood, I was wondering if I could stop by. I need to speak with you about something?"

"Is everything okay? Is something wrong with Sasha?" she asked, immediately filled with concern for the child.

"You are sweet to worry about her. But she is fine. There is just something that I want to discuss with you."

"Sounds serious," she said as she pulled out the trout and began to filet the fish.

"It may be nothing. I'll be there in a few. I hope you can take a break," he said.

Apprehension filled her as she continued to work, trying to maintain focus on the cuts of fish. He arrived fifteen minutes later and her assistant showed him to the kitchen. "Hey there. Let me clean my hands," she told him. He watched as she squeezed lemon juice on her hands, then used a hand sanitizer.

"Is there somewhere we can speak in private?" he asked with no expression on his face.

"Of course, come on in my office," Jennifer told him

with a great deal more trepidation than she was letting on. In the small office that she shared with her assistant, it also held the time clock where the staff clocked in. Shifts were about to start so there wasn't much time or much privacy. She closed the door, taking a stand behind her desk, rubbing Citrusion Body Butter on her hands to prevent drying.

"That smells amazing. What is that?" She handed him the jar from the Pilgrim Soap Company. "I like this, it's subtle and powerful." His eyes came up and he said, "Like you."

In two steps he was in front of her, so close – a bit too close for her comfort. "Jen, I can't stop thinking about you. If I don't kiss you in the next five seconds, I am going to lose my mind."

Her hand reached for the front of his shirt and pulled him forward, coming around the desk to stand toe-to-toe with him. "Well, I can't have that on my conscience, can I?"

Time stood still as he placed his arms around her waist and stood close, but was careful to not allow their bodies to touch as his lips came to hers. Gently, tenderly, pressing his mouth to hers as her mouth opened slightly, Tony's tongue slipped inside to play with hers, while he allowed his mouth to slant over hers and she moved closer to him, their thighs now touching, her fingers going into his hair. Tony deepened the kiss. Jennifer pressed her body closer. A low growl emitted from the back of his throat as a gentle knock came at the door.

"Chef Taylor, are you in there? Hiro is here with the salmon you ordered," her assistant called out.

Exhaling, she leaned into his strength, enjoying the

feel of his arms around her waist, the heat of his body against her own. "Duty calls," she whispered into his ear.

Tony pulled his head back to glance down at her face, his hand coming to her cheek, brushing the soft skin with his fingertips. "Jen," he said as he kissed her again, then reluctantly let go.

"Stay put, be right back," she told him as she opened the office door to greet the fishmonger.

Jennifer's assistant came into the office to collect a slip of paper she had no real need for, eyeing Tony with more than a mild curiosity. "You were in last week with your daughter, right? Chef Taylor is catering her party?"

"Yes, that is correct."

The assistant was being nosy. Tony didn't like nosy people. He liked even less the way the young lady was eyeing him as she sat in the chair. He was relieved when Jennifer returned to the office.

He stood as she entered the room, smiling at her. They both stared at Melinda, waiting for her to leave the office. "Oh, excuse me," she said, now somewhat bashful. The handsome man was only focused on her boss.

"Tony, I'm sorry. I don't remember why you said you were here and what you wanted to discuss," Jen said as she closed the door behind the girl.

"I told you what I needed. I need some alone time with you," he said with a fire in his eyes that began to warm her from her core outwards. He pulled her into his arms. "I need to hold you. Shower you with affection, feel your body against mine, gaze deep into those brown eyes that seem to steal my breath every time you look at me. I need you," he said as his lips trailed down her neck.

"Oh wow ... you and those pretty words," she said as

she leaned into him. "Let's get Sasha's event out of the way first, and close out that order of business. Then we can see about anything else."

Tony didn't like the sound of that. "Are you worried I won't pay you?"

"Oh, I'm getting paid?" She waggled her eyebrows at him.

"Yes, I was going to compensate you for your time," he said with a furrowed brow.

"I need to be clear on what I am trying to get done with her first. I don't want a bevy of emotions to cloud her party. You know what I mean?"

"Hell no!" His face was contorted like she had asked to borrow his underwear.

"Tony, hear me out, okay?"

"No, I don't want to hear this nonsense. I thought you and I were talking about something a bit more substantial between us. Now you push me away?"

Jennifer tried to calm him by placing a hand on his chest. "Stop it!" she told him with some force in her voice. "Kids have a sixth sense about this kind of stuff. I need to allow my time with her to be clear of sexual tension between you and me. If not, she won't trust either of us."

Tony knew what she was saying to be true. It didn't mean he had to like it. "What about what I need, Jen?"

"Your ass needs a cold shower. That's what you need! You'll be fine. You can hold it for another week or so," she told him as she kissed him briefly and opened her office door. "Have Sasha here next Thursday when she gets out of school."

"Next Thursday? I won't see you again until next Thursday?"

"Yes," she said with some reluctance. Her body wanted to see him tonight. It took everything in her not to laugh as she looked at his contorted face. Tony P was pouting.

"See you next week."

Even when he left the office, he was planning in his mind the next time they would see each other. In Raleigh, Tino Boehner was also planning the next time he would his brother Tony or even have a conversation with his mother.

Ebony sat behind the desk, staring at Tino who was covered in dirt, grime and a gigantic smile. In the past four months of dating, she had learned so much about what made him tick and what truly made him happy. Working with his hands made him happy. The meetings, managing the office and being a figurehead was the last thing that he wanted to do. Tino reveled in the high of finding a property and converting it to a livable home for a family. Based on what she had learned, family meant a great deal to him.

Right now, she had to find a way to help him slice and dice his way through this family issue with his birth mother. Still, it must be an odd feeling for him to have two mothers. "Babe," she yelled out the window. "How does next weekend sound for Atlanta?"

"Sounds good, I'll call Tony and let him know to expect us."

As he stood in the yard of the little yellow house he

had acquired, he thought it would be a great home for him and Ebony to possibly start their family together. If only he could clear away the cobwebs and the old grease in the pot on the stovetop from his own.

MENU 10

Intermezzo...

As hard as it was for her to admit, Jennifer was really looking forward to her time with Sasha. Her hormonal clock was ticking like crazy and, much like her father, she really wanted a child of her own. However, before any of that could happen, so much in her life needed to change. There was no way she could start a family and be on her feet all day in a kitchen. With more money, she could afford to hire a full time chef and she could be more of an administrator, and not so much a cook. But time would tell. In the interim, Sasha was a nice palate cleanser.

At four o'clock on the dot, Tony P walked in the door with his daughter. He carried a leather satchel with his laptop and asked for a place to set up so he could work. He really wanted to watch Jennifer do her thing. No. He really wanted to watch her. *Dear Lord, she is a lovely creature.*

"Hey there, Sasha. Grab an apron, roll up your sleeves and let's get started," Jennifer told her as she pulled out carrots, celery, radishes and broccoli bunches. "We will start with the crudités," she told the girl as she first demonstrated the sizes and layout vegetables would be in, then gave her new student several containers to place the vegetables in.

"If you have any questions, Sasha, let me know." Then Jennifer walked away, leaving the child on her own.

"Chef Jennifer, you're not going to supervise me?" Sasha asked with some surprise.

"Why? Do you need to be supervised on cutting up

some vegetables?"

"Well, when you put it that way ... I guess not," she said as she looked at the pile of produce.

"Just don't slice off a finger or anything. I'll be back and check on you in a few," she told her. She looked at Tony and shook his hand. He looked down at where their hands were touching and looked back up at her with an *are you serious* look on his face. Jennifer had to stifle her laughter. "Mr. Peay, if you like, you can use my office to set up and work."

"Why don't I just do that?" he told her with a twisted mouth as he pushed her hand away like it was covered in something nasty. This, of course, made her actually burst out in laughter, which caught Sasha's attention.

"What's so funny?" Sasha asked.

By this time, Jennifer had cleared a space for him to use her desk. She moved the old menu out of the way and placed the new menu idea and pricing on top of the pile. Jennifer responded to the girl, but kept her eyes on the father, "Just trying to make sure your dad knows where to park it."

This made Tony laugh as he lowered his voice. "I got something else I would like to park...."

She ignored him and went back into the kitchen, standing next to Sasha and watched her work.

"Here, let me help," she said as she grabbed the celery, broke down the stalks and washed them in the big sink. With a few white flour rags, Sasha watched the chef blot dry the stalks and begin to dice them.

Sasha watched her with interest until Jennifer finally said, "So you don't like Kitty Berry?"

The girl's eyes were wide. "No! I love Kitty, but my

dad and Grandma won't let me go to events like that."

"May I ask why?"

She sighed as the snipped the top off a radish and made a perfect rosette out of it and added it to the bin. "My grandma says concerts like that are patrolled by predators, and too much can go wrong real quick ... so I wasn't allowed to go. It's going to suck, too, because all of my friends will have all of these concert selfies. But it's okay."

Jennifer watched her with interest. "Why is it okay?"

The answer that Sasha provided was a defining moment in the budding relationship between Jennifer and Tony's daughter, a moment that melted her heart and made her want to forever be a part of the child's life. "Because I get to hang out and learn from you. I mean, I know most kids wouldn't care about this kind of stuff, but I want to make sure my dad eats right, and if I can learn to cook super well from a cool chef, who cares about a concert? I mean, I appreciate what you're doing for me even though we can't afford you. So, if I need to come and lend a hand on busy days, I will do that for you. You know, be there for you like you are for me."

If she could have caught her heart, she would have because it was melting and running down her sternum. The maternal clock inside her started humming and she turned to Sasha and pulled the child into her arms. "That is possibly the nicest thing anyone has ever said to me." She used her knuckles and wiped away the tears that had started to trickle and excused herself to go and make an important phone call.

Curiosity led Tony to pick up the menu and take a look at what was being offered. He held it up beside the current menu, which was pretty plain and bland. He understood the concept for a bistro, but the food wasn't plain, so the menu shouldn't be either. With his phone, he snapped a photo of the printed menu, as well as the old one, and set to work designing something worthy of the Pretentious Puss. He thought a logo of a sensual cat with full pouty lips would be perfect.

Melinda walked into the office to find him sitting behind the desk. "So whatcha working on there, big guy? The new menus?"

He could not put his finger on it, but something about Jennifer's assistant bugged the heck out of him. "Yeah, I was taking a look at it, thinking of something new to jazz it up a bit."

Before he could say boo, she was around the desk, standing so close to him, he could smell what she ate for lunch. Her voice was breathy as she told him, "You smell so good."

Sasha must have known something was wrong by the look on his face and she immediately came into the office. "Dad, I should be done in a little while, then we can leave and get home to Mom. I'm excited to tell her about the things Chef Jennifer is teaching me."

Tony stared at her with amazement. Jennifer was right – kids do have a sixth sense. Melinda straightened up. "I'm sorry, I didn't know you were married. I didn't see a ring or anything. I'm sorry."

As Melinda moved from behind the desk, Sasha came around and plopped herself on his lap. With the cutest of grins she told the nosy helper, "Yeah, he has a metal allergy, so he can't wear jewelry." It wasn't true, but ironically enough, today he wore a watch with a leather band. "I know Mom was thinking about getting you a leather band for your finger so the young ladies can stop hitting on you."

Tony was shocked at his daughter's insight, but also at how cleverly she had managed to get rid of Melinda. He said with a low voice, after Melinda had backed awkwardly out of the office, "Well, that was brilliant."

She kissed him on the cheek. "Thank me later by asking Chef Jennifer to cook us some dinner. All this food is making me hungry."

"Will do," he told her as she went back to her station and began working on the carrots.

His phone was still lying upon the desktop when it began to vibrate. "Tony Peay, how may I help you?"

The voice on the other end was almost yelling in the phone. "Hey, it seems like I am heading to Atlanta tomorrow, any way you can work me in this weekend?"

It was Tino. Tony didn't like surprises and something about this sudden desire for a visit was sitting sideways in his mouth.

"Well, this Saturday is my daughter's 13th birthday party and she is having a sleepover. So the house will be full of young girls..."

"You have a daughter?"

"Yes, she is a handful," Tony said, hoping this would give him an out.

Tino felt emotional and wanted to get off the phone as fast as possible. He had a blood related niece. "Great, I'll drop by and bring her a gift. Can you text me a time and your address? I don't plan to stay long."

For some reason that made Tony feel better. "Sure thing, see you Saturday."

Is that quail...

Life is all about timing. Whether you are in the right place at the right time, or just having a windfall arrive in the nick of time, or being completely out of it, is really all, well, a matter of timing. Jennifer arrived at the Peay home promptly at 10 a.m. with her SUV loaded to the gills – everything from fresh flowers for the display to perfectly cut fruit and a Ninja smoothie maker to set up for Sasha's birthday party. Based on her arrival, she was in time to witness her client in full meltdown mode.

"Sasha, what's wrong?"

The words that came out in between rants were more nervous energy than anything else. Jennifer understood far better than the child's father, who was trying to reason with her to no avail.

"Sasha?" Jennifer raised the inflection in her voice.

The girl jumped. "Yes, Chef?"

"My car is loaded in reverse order. What is in the rear is the first thing to set up, which are the cloths to pipe and drape the display tables. We have a lot of work to do. Will you lend me a hand so that I get everything set up the way you want it?"

She calmed down. She had something to focus on and she was on task. The relief on Tony's face was immediate. "Jen, she has been like this since she got out of school yesterday. I swear I was about to lose my mind."

In a matter of minutes, she also calmed Tony, who was given a task of firing up the grill to make burgers and dogs in the afternoon. It helped to get him out of Jennifer's hair because he was continually interrupting her every few minutes either trying to steal kisses when Sasha was in another room or he was just plain in the way.

Tony's mother arrived early, looked at the display, looked at the chef, said harrumph and was about to take a seat to supervise until he mentioned that Tino was going to stop by later. Jennifer read her reaction as discomfort bordering on almost irrational as she frowned, appeared disgusted, and grabbed her things to leave. It did not go unnoticed by her son, who followed his mother to the car to ask, "What was that about?"

"Nothing. He has just never come to Atlanta. Did he say why he wanted to see you?"

"No, not really, Mom. He only said that he would be in town and he was going to drop by. Should I have said no?"

She patted him on the arm. "No. I was just curious about the timing, that's all."

"As am I. Why are you leaving? You're acting like you want to avoid him," Tony said flatly.

"It's just been a really weird week. I'm headed home. Take lots of pictures," she told him as she revved the engine in her old car, and damn near peeled out of the driveway.

That action alone put Tony in a weird headspace in the next few hours, which miraculously sped by, even after they took a break for lunch to have burgers on the patio. It was a very calm lunch until Sasha asked, "Chef Jennifer, are you married?"

Jennifer nearly choked on her burger. "No, I am not,

Sasha."

This answer seemed to please the child, who went on to ask more personal questions like, "Do you have any kids?"

Tony was taken aback at her forthrightness. "Sasha Peay, mind your manners. That is none of your business!"

"Dad, I only asked because she is so good with me, I figured she must have a few kids of her own," the girl said in her own defense.

"It's okay, Mr. Peay. I do not have any children yet, Sasha. But I would like to have at least one." She said it more for his benefit than anything else.

The quiet was interrupted by the arrival of Raheem, whose timing was about as subtle as a rhino storming into a grocery store.

"Ain't this quaint?" he said as he rounded the corner of the house to walk up on the deck where they were dining. His eyes immediately went to Jennifer, the smoking grill and the lunch they were sharing.

Tony was happy to see his old friend and Jennifer was relieved to get away from the table before Sasha could ask any more questions.

"Uncle Raheem, come and see how pretty Chef Jennifer has set everything up," she said as she started to tug on the man's sleeve.

Jennifer stared at Tony.

Tony stared at Jennifer.

Raheem stared at Jennifer who broke the ice. "Uncle?"

Raheem asked, "Chef Jennifer?"

Tony asked, "Do you two know each other?"

"Dang, man, how many times do I have to tell you that all black people don't know each other?" Raheem told him with a frown.

"That's not what I meant and you know it," Tony said.

It was the perfect time for Jennifer to get back to the kitchen and leave the two of them alone. The conversation must have been deep because neither of them heard the doorbell. Which left Jennifer to answer the door since Sasha had run to change clothes for the fourth time.

The man at the door looked like a younger version of Tony. He was alone, handsome and smelled like a night of something wicked. Tino was the same height, had a similar build, and had a deeper complexion than Tony, but was just as sexy. Her mind was dancing as she let him in and led him to the patio. "Tony, your brother is here," she announced not thinking that he had told her he only had a sister.

Tino didn't correct her, which Tony immediately picked up on. The two men stood there, staring at each other as Sasha came out on the patio wearing a pink dress, with a gigantic bow on the top of her head. "Daddy, who is this? He looks like he could be your long lost brother."

Again, Tino didn't bother to correct her, but instead presented her with a small box he pulled from his pocket. "Happy birthday, young lady. What is your name?"

"I'm Sasha. Sasha Peay. Nice to meet you." She shook his hand and accepted the gift. "You brought me a present?" She tore open the wrapping to find a pretty pendant with a pearl in the middle.

Sasha kissed his cheek to say thank you as the awkward silence hovered. Raheem broke it and introduced himself.

"You know, you two do look like brothers ... anyone ever told you that?" Raheem asked. Tony just stared at Tino, waiting for him to deny it. But he didn't.

"I guess the quail is out the bag now..." Tino said as he took a seat.

Tony was furious. He was furious with his mother for running off and not letting him know something. He tried to tamp down the anger with Tino for his poor timing, showing up at his daughter's party with a giant ostrich egg expecting him to swallow it whole. All of these sentiments ran across his face and Tino was able to read everything his brother was thinking.

His only response was, "I just found out myself. I know nothing other than Jacqueline is my mother. I wanted to get to know you first and slowly, if possible, get to know her. I was happy to know that I also have a niece."

The doorbell rang as Sasha, who was now clad in a pink jogging suit, ran to answer it to let in the first wave of her friends. It was like watching a hoard of locusts descend on a wheat field. Within a half hour, Jennifer found herself replenishing much of the display. Several mothers also arrived with bottles of wine and immediately went to seek out Tony, but he was distracted by Tino.

Two hours into the whole affair, Sasha disappeared into her room and Jennifer had to go and find her. "Sasha, what's wrong?"

It was obvious that she had been crying. Jennifer sat on the bed beside her and wrapped her arms around the girl's shoulders, holding her close. "It can't be that bad, talk to me."

"Some of the girls are being mean. You know, they're

all showing their pictures from the Kitty Berry concert. They are being mean on purpose because they knew I couldn't go... and I mean this is my party... I don't understand...."

"Some girls are like that, Sasha, but you have to show them that they cannot ruffle your feathers. You have to put on a bold face and stand tall, show them that they can't get to you. Understand?"

"I understand," she sniffled.

"Good, because my birthday present for you should be arriving soon and I think you are going to really like it," she told the girl with pride.

Sasha flung herself into Jennifer's arms. "I hope you do have a baby soon. You are going to make an awesome mom."

That, of course, was the part that Tony walked in on. His timing could not be worse, or better, depending on which way you looked at it.

"Chef Jennifer, there is someone at the door for you," he announced.

"Perfect! My present for you has arrived," she told Sasha. Before they left her room, Jennifer checked the girls face, pinched her cheeks to balance her color and held out her hand for the child to take.

They arrived in the living room to see a young woman with an earpiece and a tablet in her hand. "Jennifer Taylor?"

"Yes, I'm Jennifer," she responded.

"We only have a few minutes, but she has allocated a photo op with the group and several individual pictures. Do you have your cameras ready?"

Jennifer looked to Tony, who ran into his office and

came back in time to see two of the largest black men he had ever seen in his life. The mothers, who had stayed and were drinking wine on the patio, all were getting concerned by the large men until Jennifer held up her hand. "It's fine, I have a special present for Sasha. No need for alarm."

The front door opened and Kitty Berry walked in. The assistant was standing next to Sasha as the pop singer walked straight to the girl. "I was told that you're one of my biggest fans, but couldn't make the concert last week, so I thought I would pop in and take a few selfies with you."

Sasha's lip was trembling as she looked at Chef Jennifer. "Thank you soooo much." Her eyes were watering as the singer draped her arm over the girl's shoulders and snapped a few selfies with her phone and then with Sasha's. She sat on the couch as the other girls surrounded her and Tony took a few group pictures promising to get them to Sasha so she could text them to everyone at the party.

The assistant gave the signal for them all to leave. Kitty looked at Chef Jennifer and said, "Anytime you are ready to come back to LA…"

Jennifer shook her hand to thank her. "No, I am good right where I am." She said it to Kitty, but her eyes were on Tony. The pop diva left as quietly as she had entered, leaving the room full of girls and parents full of questions for both Jennifer and Sasha, who stood in the middle of the fray, beaming with newfound celebrity. The girl turned her head briefly to locate where Jennifer was in the room, giving her a big grin and mouthing the words, "You are so awesome." Her eyes were full of love and

Jennifer was turning into a pile of goo.

Raheem was standing next to Tony and said really low, "I think I am falling for her, too."

Tino stepped up. "... And she can cook. I'm with him," he said as he spooned in another helping of the grits, mixed with shrimp and mushrooms. "I have never tasted grits this smooth and creamy ... and this shrimp ... and the sausage ... with mushrooms, over grits? She is impressive."

Tony was grinning as wide as his daughter. "You don't even know the half of it."

Time out....

It was an odd evening as Jennifer broke down the displays and packed up the food. She was careful to avoid contact with Raheem, who seemed to hide behind corners watching her work. Tino kept coming into the kitchen, handing her his business cards, trying to convince her to come to Raleigh. He even promised to buy her a house or give her one. She was uncertain of what he meant by that. The mothers of the daughters at the party were all begging for her number and the look on Sasha's face was unmistakable.

"Thank you so much, ladies, but I'm afraid I can't. This event was something special for Sasha alone. My calendar is completely booked. I can't do any more private parties this year," she was adamant with several of the ladies. One lady would not accept her answer until Jennifer finally said, "No. Now stop asking."

This pleased Sasha to no end and Jennifer was worried that she had created a monster. She took the time to clean all of the chafing dishes and serving pans before she loaded them into her car with some help from Tony and Tino. Raheem was still watching her as if he was waiting for the horns to sprout. Finally, with her car loaded, it was nearly 9 p.m. and it had been a very long day. Tino, finally accepting that she would not move to Raleigh, resigned himself to a to-go container of grits, loaded with everything he could find, including a separate container of birthday cake. Baking was not her thing, but Melinda was a pretty decent pastry chef, and she had created a pink Wii cake that all the children loved. Especially Sasha's BFF, Emily, who stopped several times to tell Jennifer that her food was, "Like, totally flippin' amazing!" *Well, you can't get much better than that.*

Tony was getting the girls settled with a movie before bed as Sasha found Jennifer heading out the back door. "Chef Jennifer?"

Her back was turned but she responded, "Yes, Sasha?"

The girl's face was full of emotion, her eyes were welled with tears. "If I had a mom, I would want her to be like you." She flung herself into Jennifer's arms and the tears began to drain down her cheeks.

"And if I had a daughter, Sasha. I would want her to be you," she told the girl who squeezed her tighter, nearly crushing the air out of her lungs before she quickly pulled away.

"Will I see you again, Chef Jennifer?"

Raheem stood by watching and even Tino had to turn his back for a minute to tamp down the very real emotions that were hitting him too close to home. Jennifer kissed her cheek. "Of course, let me leave you my number." She handed the girl her business card, gave a salute to the guys and headed to her car.

Tony came into the kitchen. "Where's Jen?"

Raheem pointed towards the driveway. It was obvious he was upset that she was leaving without saying goodbye, so he called after her.

"I'm back here, Mr. Peay," she told him.

In the dimly lit space between her car and his house, his approach was slow. There were so many things he wanted to say to her, but he was uncertain of what should come out of his mouth first. He started with the obvious. "Thank you for an amazing day. What you did for my daughter ... I can't even begin to ..."

She placed her hand on his chest. "She is a wonderful child. You have done an amazing job. Now, I have to get home before I drop from exhaustion."

"Jennifer ... I ..."

She held her hand up as she slid into the driver's seat of her car. "Goodnight, Mr. Peay."

"Anytime ... any place ... any moment of the day or night, I will be yours, Jennifer, you have only to give the word."

She had given her last words for the rest of the weekend, she was not up to talking to anyone about anything as she started the engine, tooted her horn and drove off. He turned back to see both Tino and Raheem peeping around the corner, nearly falling over each other trying not to be seen.

"You guys aren't hiding. You know she saw you," Tony told them.

The patio, well lit and away from eight 13-year-old girls, was the perfect place to sit and close out the evening. The silence between the three men was not uncomfortable, but there was a great deal for the brothers to talk about.

"So, is the Tino short for anything," Tony asked.

Tino watched his face. "Yes, Valentino. And Tony is short for...?"

"Short for Anthony," he said and waited.

"And our sister ... her name?"

"Cleopatra, but we call her Cleo."

Tino smiled. "So Jackie is a movie buff? Is your middle name Marc or Quinn?"

"Quinn, how did you guess?"

Tino smiled a bit. "My middle name is Rudolph." It took Tony a minute but he finally nodded that he got it. That would also explain why Cleo's middle name was Elizabeth. That was the second time it had been said that his mother was a movie buff, and honestly, until the moment, Tony felt as if he didn't know his mother at all. Tino wanted answers and truthfully he had none. He was the oldest of three children. Why their mother had given Tino away was an unknown variable, but he was going to find out.

Tino smiled at him, cognizant that Raheem had stayed as moral support for his friend in case anything went awry, but he assured them both, "I don't want to start any trouble. If my being here is worrisome for Jackie and she doesn't want me to know or to talk to me about any of it, I understand and will respect it. I am here really to establish a relationship with you, your daughter, and eventually get to know Cleo. If you don't want that either, I can respect it, as well."

Tony knew what if felt like to be rejected and he was not going to do it to Tino twice. "You are my brother. We are family. I would love to get to know you and I welcome you into our life. The other parts, we will have to take on a case-by-case basis."

"Fair enough," Tino told him.

What was not fair, clear or understandable was his mother. Admittedly, she wasn't the more affectionate of the two parents, but she was supportive. Her help with raising Sasha could not have meant more to Tony, but he was still confused about why she had given Tino away. *Maybe it was just a matter of economics.* He left it at that and gave no more thought to it.

Wild Mushrooms...

Jacqueline Boehner Peay was the epitome of a Baptist minister's daughter. She sang in the church choir, taught Sunday school to the kids, and helped out around the church. Jackie, as many called her, also ran the church lending closet. In her heart she wanted to be a jazz singer. Her silken soprano voice was enjoyed by all in the church and each week she had a solo. The good Reverend Randolph Boehner always stressed to his oldest that her voice was a gift from God and it should be used to exalt His glory. "The moment you try to use it for your own personal gains, you will fall out of His favor."

Jackie didn't listen. Every chance she got she was singing, rhythm and blues, jazz standards and some pop tunes. She wanted to be on stage, go on tour, and move to Hollywood to see her name in lights. The more her father cautioned her, the less she cared. "Jackie, I am not going to keep telling you. No good is going to come of you trying to waste your gift on worldly gains."

In an effort to quell her wanderlust, Rev. Boehner signed her up to sing with a local choir group comprised of different youth, from local churches. Jackie wasn't sure what her father had in mind, but a busload of preachers' kids on the move each weekend was a rolling busload of sin. It was true what they said that preachers' kids were the worst kind and in the back seat of the rolling bus of sanctimony is where Anthony Quinn Peay was conceived.

At 18 years old, Jackie walked across the stage to gather her diploma wearing her new wedding ring and hiding her little tummy from her friends. Isaiah Peay wasn't the most handsome of young men, but he was the first one to really pay Jackie any real attention. His father, also a minister, was disappointed in his son, whose future had now changed drastically. The money put aside for Isaiah's college was now used as a payment on a home for him and his new wife.

Rev. Boehner really had little to say to his daughter from that point forward and pretty much treated her like a pariah. Isaiah managed to attend a local community college, earning an associate degree and eventually a bachelor's degree, but divinity school was out for him, which made him resent Jackie. He loved his son, but not his wife. Much of his time was spent at the church or working on a ministry, leaving the conversation between him and Jackie cool, at best.

When Tony was about two, Isaiah began to realize he was unfair to his wife and suggested she get out for the evening and spend her time with her friends. Her friends were headed to a rap concert. "I'm not sure about this," she told Lola, her childhood friend.

"It will be fun. Lord knows you could use some fun," Lola told Jackie as they changed into stylish clothes to go out to party. Unfortunately, Lola and Jackie had two different ideas about partying, especially after they ended up in the hotel room after the concert with the rappers. It was a bad scene. Drugs on the table, liquor flowing and lots of fornicating taking place. To make it worse, Lola had disappeared and when Jackie went looking for her, she was cornered by one of the rap artist.

Most of what happened next was a blur and as much as Jackie fought, she could not stop his assault. When she opened her eyes, she noticed another man in the corner. Not sure if he was waiting his turn, she began to pray. Loud. She called on the angels on high to protect her as she cried loudly for her assailant to get off her. It must have scared them because she was let go.

She never did find Lola and she stopped looking. She took a cab home and scrubbed her skin until it was almost red, trying to wash away the sin of another man touching her in such a way. She felt dirty. She could not make eye contact with Isaiah, let alone stand the thought of him touching her unclean body. He took it as rejection and accepted the normal two-year missionary assignment as Chaplain that would have come with his divinity degree.

The angels must have heard her cries because she had conceived a child from the assault. She hid it as best she could and her mother, a very solemn woman who obeyed her husband's every command, helped her daughter hide the problem. The resemblance between the two boys was noticeable, but Tino was darker, and the texture of his hair was different. The main issue was that Isaiah had not touched Jackie in a long time and, unless it was a miraculous conception, there would be no explaining it to her husband.

"Jackie," her mother told her, "God don't make no mistakes. This child was conceived for a reason."

"Momma, the man forced himself on me. I know that was not in God's plan for me to be raped!" Her mother slapped her face.

"You will not be blasphemous, young lady," she told her daughter. "I have an idea."

If ever there was a resourceful woman, it was Ruth Biggs Boehner. She knew for a fact her niece-in-law had just gotten the news that she could not have children. "Your cousin, Tom, has just gotten a job in Raleigh and they're leaving tomorrow. We will get to the house early, bundle up little Tino and ring the doorbell."

"You want to just leave this child on their doorstep? Momma, we could at least ask her if she is willing to be a mother and take this on."

"She was devastated by the news that she could not have her own. They have been married for four years and Tom wants a son. He will have one." It was said with such command that Jackie followed along. Inside the basket was a note and the birth certificate for 18-month-old Valentino Rudolph Boehner.

"Love him, nurture him, and raise him right."

Tom never asked any questions, but took the boy as his own and raised him with love. As he grew, Jackie made a point of being there for the significant points in his life, watching him grow. The last time she saw him, he had just finished college and was an accomplished man with a love of old school music. She even heard him singing once and knew he had inherited her voice.

Irony is like a field of wild mushrooms, some you can digest, and some will make you trip out. If her life were anything close to the magic of living in a Smurf village among the wild fungi, fate would laugh at her. The one child she gave away was more like her than the two she raised in her own home.

Now a widow and a grandmother of one, her life was still empty of any of the meaning she sought. Her singing wasn't even done in the church pews anymore, and smiling was something in her past. Tino was coming into their lives and at some point she had to tell him the truth – no matter how painful it was for either of them. She would not ask his forgiveness because in her mind, there was nothing to forgive – he was raised with love by a man he called father and another woman he called mother.

It was better than being raised in a house with a man that would have resented, if not hated him.

A Wild Wednesday...

"Hello, this is ..." she looked at the caller on her cell. It was Tony. Today was Wednesday and her off day. She was dirty, tired, and her muscles were screaming for a massage, which is where her afternoon was going to be spent. After she got up off the couch.

And took a shower.

And had something to eat.

Maybe wash her hair.

"I woke up thinking about you and that beautiful ass of yours," he almost growled into the phone.

She laughed, "Tony, is this a booty call?"

"Yes. Yes, it is. That booty is calling my name," he said with a lowered sexiness in his voice. "Bring me some, right now, or I will come and get it. Either way, I need you."

That was a better idea than what she had in mind for the afternoon. "No, you can't come to me. I live at home with my dad, remember? He is headed out to golf, but I never know when he will be back."

"Come to me. Sasha is at school. I'll call my sister and ask her to pick her up and take her to her house afterwards so you and I can have some much needed alone time," he said with such an edge in his voice that she could almost feel the pull of him.

"Okay, it will be about an hour, though," she told him as she looked in the mirror at her saddened state.

"I can't wait that long...."

"I have to shower and wash my hair," she said with

some sternness in her voice.

"I will take it dirty. Make it fifteen."

"A half hour is the best I can do."

"Good, see you in ten. Any longer than that, I may start and finish without you." The bass of his laughter rumbled in his chest.

"I will be there as soon as I can," she told him before hanging up. Jennifer did a shimmy in her bedroom mirror and began to hum as she made her way into the kitchen to grab a cup of coffee before jumping in the shower.

Her dad was at the kitchen table watching her. "I know that tune. That is an 'I'm going to get some' tune. I want to meet him. And soon, Jenny." He said it without looking up from his paper.

"Daddy, I don't know what you are talking about," she said, trying to play innocent.

He still never looked up. "I want to meet the future father of my grandson before anything goes any further. You hear me, girl?"

How does he know these things? "Daddy, seriously, I don't know how you come up with these sweeping conclusions."

As Jennifer turned around to face old Johnny Taylor, the paper was down and his eyes were on her. The deadpan look on his face was very similar to when she came home tipsy, lied and said she hadn't been drinking and then tumbled over a basket in the hallway.

"You met him the night of your class reunion. You also spent Sunday with him and now, you are going to meet him again. Like I said, I want to meet this man before anything goes much further," he told his daughter.

Again. How does he know these things?

"Daddy, we're not that serious," she told her father.

"Then your clothes should stay on. If they are coming off, again, then I want to meet him before it goes any further." His facial expression had not changed.

"I don't think we are anywhere close to being..."

He held up his hand. "The minute you decided to get into bed with him, he became a part of your life. I need to know if he is serious about you. If he's not, then he and you both need to move on. You are too old to be playing house. Either you are looking for a mate and father of your children, or you need to get your butt back in church and ask the good Lord to send you a life partner."

It wasn't up for discussion. Johnny had spoken and he left the room to make sure she understood the conversation was over. So was her desire for sex. Yet she told Tony she was coming over and she would keep her word.

Tony felt like a kid at Christmas. He didn't know what to do first. *The bed. Start with the bed.* He changed the sheets and loaded the dirty ones in the wash before coming back to turn down the bed. Since he didn't have any roses, and Jen was a chef, he ran to the backyard and grabbed some lemongrass, rosemary and lavender and threw on the sheets.

Not wanting to feel like a pig of seismic proportions, he pulled out a bottle of sparkling cider, put it on ice, dipped some strawberries in a quick melting chocolate, sliced up some pineapple, pulled out a wedge of Gouda, opened some Brie, and added some crumbled bleu cheese to a tray. Thank goodness his daughter didn't like junk. This was the good stuff and it was a nice looking presentation. "Crackers ... I need crackers." He wished he had some caviar, but this would have to do in a pinch. The more the clock ticked, the more crazed he became, his need for her nearly poking a hole in his pants. In his current state, all she would need to do was to rub up against him twice and he would be 15 all over again. By the time he heard the car door slam, he had to untuck his shirt.

Calm, Tony. Calm.

How can I be calm? I've never had a woman over. Not even on the weekends Sasha slept over at my mom's.

He opened the door before she rang the bell. "Hello, you," she told him as she walked by, smelling like a moving dinner entree to a pack of hungry wolves. Her fingers grazed across his abdomen. She would do her best to play hard to get, but really, she wanted to drop every stitch of clothing and prostrate herself in the middle of his bed.

His hand slipped into hers as he closed and locked the door and led her into the living room. "Before anything happens, Jennifer, I need you to know my intentions are pure and gentlemanly."

It was obvious he was nervous as he kept shifting his weight from foot to foot. She felt inclined to ask as she kicked off her shoes, "Why the codicil?"

The cheese and cracker display caught her eye. "Very nice, Tony."

"I'm glad you like it. It may be 30 to 45 minutes before

you even get to taste a morsel," he told her with a wicked smile. Her eyebrows went up.

"Again, my intentions are not going to match my actions," he said as he pulled her into his arms. "It's been a month. A month of longing, needing, craving your touch, Jen."

Tony's lips touched hers and sparks begin to fly. Jennifer tried to hold him off with her hand. "Tony, aren't we going to at least talk a bit before ..."

"Oh, I plan to give you a thorough tongue lashing," he said into her mouth, as his tongue darted in between her lips. His hands went to work and her dress went up, her undies went down and so did he. She was on her back on the couch, her legs peddling an imaginary bike trying desperately to put on the brakes, but he was in go mode. In between his mouth, bringing her pleasure, he managed to get his shirt off and his pants down. Jennifer was reaching for pillows or anything she could hold on to but the pleasure he was bringing her was so intense, so enjoyable, she wasn't sure what to do. He knew exactly what came next. Tony moved so fast, he was on the floor and she was straddling his lap and he had started to connect their bodies.

"Wait ... wait ... hold on ... we need protection," she cried as she tried to pull away.

"I put it on when I heard you pull up. Now, stop talking," he pulled her forward and incrementally connected them. His breathing was labored as he gripped her hips and lifted and lowered her until she felt she was going to burst.

"You feel so amazing ... I can't wait ... for you ..." he told her as his hands moved faster along with his hips.

He called her name as he squeezed her body close to his, holding her tight. Jennifer held onto to him, only experiencing the initial start of her ascent.

Tony stroked her hair as she looked at his face. The look of satisfaction covering his expression was like he had just confessed all of his sins. His fingers touched her lips. "You are so beautiful, Jennifer." He kissed her lightly, then stared into her eyes. "I know it's not real, yet, but kiss me and tell me you love me."

Her fingers ran through his hair, pushing it back from his brow. "That was really good ... and fast ... but I wasn't finished."

"Seven minutes, I can keep you busy for seven minutes. Two are already gone," he told her as he stared at her lips.

Jennifer stared into his eyes, kissing each eyelid, then the tip of his nose. "If that's the case, Tony P, do you know how much I love you?" Her lips met his as she deepened a kiss between them that spoke to Tony's soul.

It was all the encouragement he needed as he struggled to his feet, holding her in his arms, kicking off his pants that were trapped around his ankles and making his way to the bedroom. She loved the rosemary on the sheets, and appreciated the lavender petals as he made quick work in the bathroom.

"Take off that dress, please, so that I don't tear it up," he told her as he came back from the bathroom, completely nude and ready to continue. She stood at the bedside, removing her bra, as he stood in the precipice of the bathroom, simply taking her all in. "You are the most magnificent creature I have ever had the pleasure of laying my eyes on. Your inner beauty outshines the outer, and I am losing myself in you."

"Well, you silver-tongued devil, let me help you completely fall off the edge of reality," she told him and lay on the bed, opening herself to him.

Most women understand that there is a difference between making love and having sex. Where Tony P took Jennifer next was somewhere above the realms of both worlds and held her there on a cloud of euphoria. His movements were strategic as each touch, each stroke, each kiss elevated the connection between them. If he was trying to make a point, he was doing a fantastic job. He asked her to let go and give in to where he was leading her and by following his instructions, he would take her somewhere she had never been. She let go.

Jennifer stopped thinking.

The past hurts of poor choices she released.

The unshed tears for former heartbreaks she folded in half and ripped to pieces as he lifted her body to a higher place.

Manacles that had chained her heart were opened, melted and the keys tossed into the abyss of nothingness where she had been hiding for almost two years. As he whispered encouraging words in her ear, face down on the bed, with a pillow under her hips and fabric of the sheets clutched in her hands, she splayed open her fingers, stretched out her toes and dove off the platform he provided into the unknown.

It was powerful.

It was freeing.

It was beautiful.

She called out his name at the top of her voice as hot tears ran down her face, while she rode the crescendo.

She balled up her fingers and gripped on tight to the mattress as his movements became more forceful. He was reaching his critical moment, grunting her name and holding a handful of her hair, reaching the twinkling of his ecstasy. Tony's face was contorted and he climbed up the crest, lost in the world where only the two of them existed and he let go to join her in the magical world he had created. It was so surreal, but in the background, and there it was... a scream.

He slowed his movements, leaning forward to whisper in her ear, "Jen, are you okay? Am I hurting you?"

It wasn't Jennifer who screamed.

They looked up, and there in the doorway stood Sasha with a look of horror on her face.

Based on the look of rage on her father's face, the handful of hair her father had in his hands, and the tears rolling down Chef Jennifer's face, Sasha thought this couldn't be normal sex.

"Daddy, stop it! You're hurting Chef Jennifer!"

Say what now...

Life has a way of coming at you so fast, it builds and uncertainty of whether turning left or right will put you in harm's way. Sometimes, in order to handle a crisis, you have to point your life in the direction of the oncoming maelstrom and tackle everything head on. There was no way of dancing about and easing into letting Sasha know he was interested in seeing Jennifer. His opportunity to invite her over for a cozy little family dinner and ease her into their lives was shot. Tony P's worst fear had just played out and he was terrified that he had lost his daughter's respect. How he handled this scenario was going to be a life changing moment for all three of them.

Tony was ready for his life to change.

As he and Jennifer scrambled to cover themselves, his voice was calm as he asked Sasha to wait for them in the living room. Thank goodness he was composed in the middle of all of this because Jennifer was mortified. She could not get dressed fast enough and she wanted to simply slink out of the window and never see him or his child again. She managed to get dressed. Her clothes were crooked, her hair was a mess and her lipstick was all over the bottom portion of her face. *I just need my shoes ... and my panties. Where in the hell are my panties?*

Tony noticed she was frantic as he placed his hands on her shoulders, then straightened her dress, and used his thumb to wipe away the smudged lipstick. "Jen, we have nothing to be ashamed of. We've done nothing wrong other than forgetting to lock my bedroom door." He mashed down her hair before slipping his hand into hers and pulling her down the hallway to meet a very upset 13-year-old. A 13-year-old who held Jennifer's discarded underwear at the end of a writing pen. Jennifer mumbled thanks as she used the guest bathroom to put them on, as well as to comb her hair down.

Tony took a seat on the overstuffed love seat and suggested Sasha sit as well. "I'm sorry you had to see that. Obviously, I wasn't expecting you to be home."

"Aunt Cleo couldn't pick me up, so I took the bus home," she told him. Her face was full of anger and he didn't understand why.

"Sasha, why are you so angry?" He really wanted to know. Sasha's gaze was fixed on Jennifer as she returned from the bathroom and took a seat at the far end of the couch. Away from them both.

"Are you okay, Chef Jennifer? I mean you were crying, and Daddy was pulling your hair…." Her face was full of confusion.

Jennifer wanted the floor to open and chew her into tiny pieces before spitting her out and chucking her across an open field full of ravenous mice.

Tony leaned forward as he asked incredulously, "Jen, you were crying?"

This can't be happening to me. I should have listened to my daddy. "I'm okay, both of you. I had a moment…."

If she hadn't been looking at him, and witnessed it for herself, she would not have believed it. She actually saw Tony's chest swell with pride. Sasha saw it, too, and frowned at her father. Then the questions began to fly, each worse than the last.

"How long has this been going on between you two?"

was the first, but neither could answer because they were too stunned by the second question.

"Was my daddy giving you a baby?" This made Jennifer spring to her feet.

"Are you two in love?" Tony was stammering but neither was prepared for the next question.

"I know what this is ... you two planned that whole birthday thing to get me to like Jennifer so you two could trick me. You're going to ship me off to boarding school so you can start a new family! Without me!" Her eyes were wide and Jennifer grabbed her purse and shoes. *Fail. Fail. Going downhill fast.*

"I will just leave and never come around again. I'm sorry, Sasha. So sorry." She clutched her things and literally ran for the door. But Tony was on his feet and grabbed her arm.

"Oh no you don't! I am not going through this by myself. Get back in here," he told Jennifer as the three of them sat, each staring at each other, Tony, back on the love seat and the two of them on the couch.

"I have enough love for both of you and I plan to lavish you both with it," he said flatly. Over the next thirty minutes, Tony P reassured his daughter and Jennifer as well. His voice was steady as he spoke of his loneliness and the joy that he was experiencing simply being able to talk to Jennifer each day. It came as no surprise when he told his daughter that he was happy that she and Jennifer had hit it off, but it was not a ploy of some sort. "We both wanted your party to be a success and it was."

Sasha was listening closely to everything he was saying. Jennifer had a flashback to her childhood when she ran off Ms. Jackson, who was in their kitchen, coming on to her father. Now she knew how that lady must have felt. She still said nothing, even after he asked her a question. Twice.

"Jennifer? Did you hear me?"

In truth she had not. She was still in his bed, covered in shame. "I'm sorry, what did you say?"

"I wanted to know if you were okay to move forward with me and Sasha and have *us* be a part of your life?" He said it with a look on his face that was asking for something more. *My acceptance of him? Acceptance of what?*

She smiled at him and Sasha. Here it is. The same thing her daddy had said earlier this morning. *If you are going to sleep with him, you need to be serious about him.* Her focus on Tony now changed because her daddy was right. Could she see this man as her husband and the father of her children?

She swallowed hard and had to say what was needed. No beating around the bush, she opened her mouth and let the words roll out. "Only if you are open to the possibility of having more children and if Sasha is okay to have more brothers and sisters in the future." Her eyes were wide as she waited for his rejection and sending her and her panties packing.

Tony didn't miss a beat. "I'm okay with it. Sasha, are you?"

Sasha nearly made Jennifer choke on her own saliva. "I dunno. If that's how you make a baby, you sure you want to do that again, Chef Jennifer?"

Jennifer's hands went to her face, her skin warming by the second. Sasha stood up to go to the kitchen. "If that is what sex is like, then I'm NEVER having any!"

Tony called after her, "From your mouth to God's ears, young lady!"

He looked at Jennifer and it appeared as if all the color had drained from her face. He rose from the loveseat and pulled her into his arms. "The ugly part is over, Jen. Now we just figure out how to move forward." He kissed the top of her head. "I guess next you need to have us over for dinner to meet your family."

Jennifer pulled back so she could get a gaze at his face. A face that was getting blurry. "Say what now?" Her knees began to buckle and she went limp in his arms.

She had passed out.

MENU 16

Beefing it up...

"See, Daddy, you broke her," Sasha said as she ran to get a cool cloth to place on Jennifer's forehead. She was dizzy because she hadn't eaten and her blood sugar had dropped. Her hands were shaking, her stomach roiling and Tony Peay had just agreed to be the father of her children. Unfocused eyes looked at Sasha. If all went well, this would be her daughter. *Dear Lord, what am I doing?*

Jennifer still did not know what had happened to the girl's mother. "I'm sorry. I just haven't had a chance to eat anything today, and so many emotions in such a short period of time...." It was all too much.

Tony gave her some orange juice along with the cheese and crackers before she headed home. The drive to her childhood home was filling the space in her head of what to do next. *How do I tell my daddy that I am seeing a white man with a child?* Her father was the least of her worries. It was Wednesday afternoon and he always has a 10:30 tee time. It was now after 3 pm; he could still be out for at least another hour in the clubhouse, talking trash with his friends.

Instead, she slipped into the back door to find her sister, Gloria, at the table. "You look like you've been rode hard and put away wet. Emphasis on the rode hard," she told her over the rim of wired spectacles. And they were spectacles.

Gloria Taylor had a style of her own. A kind of Angela Davis meets Coffy Brown; afro included. Gloria wore natural hair before it became a statement of the new American black woman. She was an entrepreneur and a women's rights advocate who ran a small independent publishing house and literary publication. On weekends she hosted an open mic poetry slam in the bottom of her office building that also served as her home. When she was not at their dad's, and as far as anyone knew, Gloria was single. She had never invited anyone home to meet her family and her relationship with Jennifer had always been cool. Not as in they were cool. More like can we get some heat turned on in here, cool.

Jennifer hated that and she wanted it to change but didn't know where to start or how. So she took the high road. "I had a really messed up afternoon, Gloria, and I am at a loss of what to say or where to go from here."

Gloria looked over her shoulder to see if someone else had walked into the room and her baby sister was addressing them. Jennifer had never confided in her, let alone asked her advice about anything, so this was truly new territory for them both. "Okay, little sis, what is troubling you?"

Jennifer began to explain it all. The reunion, the bar, the kid helping in the kitchen, the party, and this afternoon, including Sasha's reaction. Gloria had started to chuckle midway through the whole recitation, but, by the end, she was folded over in gut-busting laughter.

"Oh shit, that ain't nothing. I had my girl's son walk in on us. You talk about confusing!" Gloria said, still trying to stop the laughter that was welling inside of her. She changed the subject and suddenly turned serious when she saw her younger sister wasn't amused and really in need of some advice. "Jenny, it sounds like he manned up and handled his daughter and you, as well. He said he was ready to be a father to your children and sounds like you are ready to be a mother to his daughter."

"Yeah, but I don't know what happened to her mother. It's all so new and moving so fast. It's only been a month," Jennifer said as she laid her head on the kitchen table.

"Well, slow it down and find out," she said as she patted her sister on the head. "And he said he wants to come here and meet me and Daddy?"

Jennifer's head was still down and on the table. She bobbed her head yes as Gloria stated, "Great, I'm free on Sunday. Let's do it then."

"Did I mention he was white?" she said to her sister with her face still kissing the table.

Gloria jumped up and started running around the kitchen hooting. "Oh hell yeah! I will be here. Bright and early."

Jennifer raised her head, shaking it no.

Her sister was bobbing her tight afro up and down, "Oh yeah. I can't wait, Jenny. A reverse guess who's coming to dinner? This is going to be too good."

Then she was hit with a brilliant idea. "I'll invite them Sunday for dinner if you bring your girl."

Gloria stopped laughing. Jennifer stuck her hand out for a shake. "Deal?"

"No. I wasn't part of this equation. Ain't no deal!"

"I will go you one better, big sis. I'll even put you together a tray of food for your Saturday night poetry slam ... if you bring your special lady on Sunday to dinner," Jennifer said, knowing it would reel her in.

"You will cater my poetry slam on Saturday?" Gloria

asked incredulously.

"No, I will provide you with a chafing dish with some meatballs on one side, some wings on the other and a tray of veggies with some dip," Jennifer clarified.

They stood in the kitchen, staring at each other, when their father walked in through the back door. He looked at Gloria first, then at Jennifer, who looked pretty rough. He wanted to say something, but was uncertain what they were in the midst of ... a fight?

"Ladies," he said with some hesitation.

Jennifer took the lead, still staring at Gloria. "Daddy, we're having guests for dinner on Sunday. I'll bring Tony and his daughter to meet you and Gloria is bringing her significant other."

Johnny Taylor was never a man to mince words. "Did my doctor call and tell y'all I'm dying or something?"

Sharing news with your family about your personal life is always difficult, especially when you are uncertain how the changes you were planning to make will be accepted. It's not as if your changes will directly impact who and what they are, but oddly enough, many react as if it will. Any conversation with Jacqueline Peay felt that way.

At times, Tony would avoid any conversation with her about personal choices and changes in his life. Well, there hadn't been any real changes in 12 years, but the last few seemed to rock his mother to the core. He and his sister both felt that communicating with the woman was like standing on the South Rim of the Grand Canyon yelling to the North Rim about what was happening in their lives. No matter how much he tried to talk, it appeared easier to simply fill the canyon with dirt, a teaspoon of loose soil at a time. There was a great deal of loose soil hanging about and it was time to make use of it, or at least try to squeeze some sense out of it.

It was now Thursday. Tino had come to town on Saturday. His sister was supposed to pick Sasha up from school yesterday, but instead sent a message for the child to ride the bus home. Cleo confessed that she had to run to see about their mother, who was complaining of being dizzy. A little tidbit she had failed to tell him about, hence, the very severe episode of *coitus interruptus* and potentially scarring his daughter for life. He tried to handle it well, but there was so much flying at them at once. He didn't want Jennifer scared off, but he always didn't want his daughter traumatized.

"Mom," he said as he brought her a cup of tea. "Is everything okay? Cleo said you were experiencing some dizziness yesterday."

"Yes, I just had a moment and I couldn't seem to get it together to get out of the house," she said as she stared into the cup.

In his childhood, he could remember several of her episodes when she was unable to get it together. The stints would last anywhere from a couple of hours to, one time, a couple of months. Ironically, she seemed to get better once their father died. The bouts became fewer and the birth of Sasha gave her something new to focus on. Her granddaughter she seemed to lavish with love and attention. Something she rarely did with them as children. This was not to say that she was a bad mother, nor a neglectful one, just cool. Dinner was always on time. The house was always clean. Laundry was always done, and the fridge was always full with home cooked meals. If he could put his finger on the perfect description of his mother, she was like a Stepford wife. Anything out of sorts put her out of sorts. Tino had put her out of sorts.

Yet, in Tony's mind, family was everything to him, but so much needed to be sorted out. He was about to embark on a new journey in his life and he needed to beef up his relationship with his family before he brought Jennifer into it. No matter how you sliced the roast, Tino was still on the side and not part of the main course. "Mom, is this about Tino?"

Her eyes were distant as she searched his face. She gave no answer.

"He said if his arrival causes you any undue pain, he won't bother you, but he would like to get to know you," Tony told her with a low voice.

Jacqueline jumped up from the couch, spilling her tea and breaking the cup. She looked as if she wanted to take off running, but was uncertain in which direction to flee. Tony pulled her into his arms, resting her head against his broad chest. "It's okay, Mom. If you're not ready to tell him anything you don't have to. He will understand."

Her voice was low. "Why now, Anthony? Why has he come forward now? All these years, and now ..."

Tony could almost feel the thudding of her heart as he held her close. "Because he is seeing someone special and he wants to introduce her to his whole family, Mom." He took a deep breath. *Now is as good a time as any.* "I'm seeing someone as well whom I would like you to meet."

She pulled away from him, with squinted eyes, staring at him. "You're dating that chef that did Sasha's party?"

"Yes, I am. How did you know?"

The frown on her face was one of disgust. "I saw how you were looking at her with lust in your eyes."

Lust. Well, it probably was. "It's something much more than lust, Mom. I am looking to make her a permanent part of our lives?"

"Lust and fornication will not make a good marriage, Anthony Quinn Peay. And you do not have a good track record with women," she said as she shook her finger at him.

He was shocked. "What track record with women? There was a girl in high school and Sasha's mother. There haven't been any women," he told her. At least none who were permanent.

Jacqueline flopped down on the couch. *Who am I to judge?* Her emotions were all over the place. "Will I get more grandbabies to love and care for?"

He sat beside her, looking at her tentatively and worrying too much about the mood swing. "Yes, from me and Tino, probably." She jumped when he said his name.

"Between you and the chef and Tino, I am going to have a house full of little black grandbabies," she said with a flat face.

Tony stared at her in disbelief. Was she implying...? He had noticed Tino's coloring, but thought it was a really good tan.

"Mom, is Tino's father a black man?"

She began to rock back and forth on the couch, hugging herself and retreating into that dark place where she would hide from them and the world. Tony was not going to allow her to leave the table without first cleaning her plate. "Mom, stay with me. Talk to me."

"He raped me," she said as the light in her eyes dimmed. Jacqueline had withdrawn to her dark place.

Garden Salad...

Sometimes, no matter how much dressing you put on a salad, it is still a pile of vegetables with a sprinkling of crunchy nuts. Asking someone to be a part of something that was guaranteed to flush your colon was a difficult task, but Tony P had waited patiently for many years for the right woman to come along. She wandered into that bar and looked him in the eyes and said I need you to be my man. Everything in him responded to her soft plea. Whether it was what he had prayed for or if it was just something he was hopeful about, she was there.

Once he held her in his arms on the dance floor she felt right. In his hotel room, she was the perfect fit. Being exactly what he needed when he needed it was even better. He had no doubts in his mind that Jennifer Taylor was the woman for him. It was now a matter of time to make those words he often asked her for to become real. Starting today, he would work on making a life with her – a very happy one filled with love and affection. The children they would have would grow up in a house filled with love and friendliness. After speaking with his mother yesterday, he was in dire need of a hug. He knew just the woman to give him a cuddle and who also made his pants feel tight and his heart all squishy.

It was just before lunch when he pulled into the parking lot of the Pretentious Puss and parked next to her Chevy. In his hand was a folder of his preliminary layout of her new menu for summer and his ticket to walk through those doors. The jangling of the doorbell had her come from the behind the bar to greet him with that smile that made his pulse race. "Hey, you," she said casually as if she were about to buy T-shirts at the flea market.

"Hey back," he said as his eyes wandered to that beautiful mouth that he loved kissing. He held up the folder.

"What you got there, Tony P?" she asked as she eyed the manila file.

"It will cost you a kiss to see what's inside," he said playfully.

He watched her walk slowly over to him and grab the front of his shirt, pulling him forward. "Are you telling me you only want one?"

He could not stop the grin that covered his face as he moistened his lips with the tip of his tongue, getting his puckers kissing ready. "Yep, just one."

Jennifer leaned in closer and placed a big, noisy, wet kiss on his cheek and bounded backwards grabbing the folder at the same time. "There ya go!"

She was giggling as she held the file folder, waving it like a fan. Tony stood stil, simply watching her, his chest swelling with pride that she had chosen to give herself to him, twice. A slow smile crept across his face. "You are so lovely. I ..." He stopped speaking.

Jennifer's mouth was twisted as they gazed at each other. She spoke first. "You know, tomorrow is my Saturday off and I was wondering ..." Jennifer nibbled on her bottom lip. "... If I could take you on a date?"

His eyebrows shot up. "You? Take me on a date? Shouldn't that be the other way around?"

She tried her best to remember what it was like to be and feel sexy. Tony made her feel alive, but she still had to work on her sexiness. She pulled out of her repertoire of sexy moves, or what little she had left, and moved towards him slowly, the tip of her tongue stuck in the corner of her mouth. "I made the first move in that bar ..."

"And I finished the evening," he said, still rooted to his spot. Jennifer was not going to let up. If they were to have a future, like he said the first night they met, she needed to be comfortable with his touch. In the open. Where everyone could see. Especially her dad and her sister.

"I don't know how this one will finish, but I want you and Sasha to come over for dinner on Sunday to meet my dad and my sister," she said as she fingered the buttons on his shirt.

He toyed with a strand of her hair that had come from under her chef's headscarf. "Saturday night can't be too late. I have to teach Sunday school."

That was not what she was expecting to hear. "You teach Sunday school?"

"Yes, every Sunday since I was 15. Then after church, I go to my mom's and have lunch with her." He said it for two reasons. The first was that he needed to gauge her reaction, and secondly, he wanted her to know that this was something he would want her to become a part of as well.

It was unsaid, but Jennifer knew what he was implying. "Sundays are my day off, like I said before. I mean, I don't teach Sunday school, but I am in church with my dad on most Sundays, then an early supper."

Tony was still twirling the strand of hair in his fingers. "So where are you taking me on this date Saturday night?"

"I'm still thinking about it. I plan to surprise you," she told him.

Tony pretended to be girly, batting his lashes. "What should I wear? Something sexy? A suit? A tie?"

"Be comfortable." Then she remembered the folder in her hand. "What is this?" She opened the manila file and saw the newly designed menu and the beautiful colors along with the logo of a pretentious cat. Her mouth dropped. "You did this for me?"

The joy in her eyes was all he needed. "That feeling that you are experiencing... that is how I feel every time I am with you."

Her eyes drifted up from the papers to his face. "Wow, you are good," she said with a grin.

"Yes, I am. And now you know, too," he grinned at her. "Jennifer, I will give you a good life. We will be good together."

"I know, Tony. I have no doubts about it." And truth be told, she didn't. She only needed to figure out how to make it all work.

His hand went to her cheek. "Anytime ... any place ... any moment of the day or night, I will be yours," he told her.

When Tony arrived home, he was surprised to find his sister, Cleo, waiting for him. She had that look on her face where he had either done something to tick her off or she wanted to talk to him about Sasha. Cleo was a special sort of woman who was more like their mother than either woman cared to admit. His sister was more vocal about her emotions and her sense of right and wrong, whereas his mother would say one sentence and give you that look. Unlucky for him, Cleo started by giving him that look, then chose more than one sentence to try and guilt him into seeing things her way. He hated that. He never gave in out of principle, but she still continued to try.

"I went by Mom's this morning and she was in one of her states. I had to get her cleaned up and get her into some fresh clothes," she said as she gave him *that* look. He knew the next question and he was thinking of the right words to explain where they were in this impasse called Valentino.

"Yes, we had a talk yesterday. Mom is going to need to have some professional counseling," he said flatly.

"We have counseling set up at the church ..." she started to say. Also like their mother had been, Cleo was married to the pastor of their church. His father had taken it over after their father, Isaiah, had retired. Waldo Jones was a dull man with little to no imagination. Not only in his sermons, but also in life. He never even saw the humor in Cleo's name after she married him, as she became Cleopatra Jones. He only commented, "Never saw the movie." Tony couldn't complain. The man was good to his sister, as well as to Sasha.

"Cleo, for what our mother has experienced, she needs to be guided back by a professional counselor," he told her.

Always the church first lady, Cleo was adamant. "The only thing she needs to guide her back is Jesus!"

"She can't be guided back to Jesus if she can't see Him,

Cleo. Mom needs to have her path cleared first before she makes the journey," he said as he stared at her face. It was the first time she didn't argue with him. "She underwent something horrific and she never told anyone."

Cleo's mouth was twisted in disbelief. "What could be so horrible? The woman barely left the house except to go to church, the fabric or grocery store. Until Daddy started taking us out on Sundays after church, she never went to restaurants. She made all her clothes, and mine. She let Daddy shop for you. I think she is just being overly dramatic to get attention because she is lonely."

His sister was stubborn. That trait she took from their father. And it did not matter how much was placed before her, she still would only pick and choose what she believed she knew well. Even when they went out to eat at those horrible all you can eat buffets their daddy was so fond of, she still would only have a garden salad sprinkled with sunflower seeds. He ruefully acknowledged the obvious – that, like her husband Waldo, his sister had no imagination.

Tony was about to jolt her into reality. "We have a brother. His name is Valentino. He is two years younger than me and two years older than you. He is looking forward to meeting you. Also, I am seeing someone. I plan to marry her and she is black. Oh yeah," he paused to drive home how much she did not know. "So is our brother."

He left Cleo in his kitchen as she stood there, her mouth opening and closing like a fish gasping for air. It was the wrong way to tell her but sometimes he was just fed up with her thinking she knew it all. The other really ugly part he would never divulge to Tino or to his sister.

And he would roast in hell before he allowed any of those women in the church to know such a horrendous thing had happened to their mother, nor would he allow his sister to make their mom the topic of conversation at the local church social.

From what he had seen in Jacqueline Peay's behavior, she had been victimized enough.

Puffed Pastry...

It had been so long since Tony had been on a date, he didn't quite know what to do or where to start. He knew he needed a haircut and possibly a new shirt. He was at a real loss. He hadn't dated in years and his clothing, he also feared was out of date. Since he worked from home, he really wasn't keenly aware of the latest trends or men's fashion. He would purchase new suits for church, but those types of things have been never in or out of fashion. He called Raheem.

"Hey. I need your help," he told his longtime friend.

"Sure, what's up?"

"I have a date tonight with Jen and I have nothing to wear," he said solemnly. "I mean I normally just go to Penny's or Sears and get something, but I dunno... I guess I want to wear something hip and cool."

Raheem was smiling. It was good to see his friend excited about something in his life. Lord knows it had been a long road. "Where are you taking her?" Raheem asked him.

"I'm not sure where we're going. Actually, she is taking me out," he confessed.

"I like this woman. I like her a lot!" he told Tony as he grabbed his keys and headed for the door. "I'll be there in 15 minutes."

Jennifer was in the kitchen loading the serving pans for Gloria's event when her sister walked through the back door. It was already five and she still had to shower and get dressed for her date with Tony. She was grinning as she covered the pans of chicken and meatballs. *I have a date.*

"I know that look. You must be planning to get you some tonight," Gloria said as she uncovered the meatballs and stole one. She popped one in her mouth and her eyes rolled up in her head. "That is so good, I almost want to kiss you."

Jennifer stood still. Gloria wasn't very affectionate and it felt weird, but Jennifer grabbed her big sister and placed a sloppy kiss on her cheek.

Gloria wiped the slobber from her jaw as she sheepishly eyed her little sister. "Are you in love, Jennifer?"

She shook her head slowly. "If I'm not, whatever this is sure feels pretty darned good. Gloria, he is so amazing." She grabbed the folder off the counter and opened it, showing her the new menus. "He made these for me without me even asking," she told her.

"I love the logo, and these are nice," Gloria said.

"So is he. I can't wait for you and Daddy to meet him tomorrow," she told her sister as she bounced up and down like a kid about to get some ice cream.

"Why not bring him by the poetry slam tonight?"

Just like that, Gloria had sucked all the joy out of her

day. That was the last thing she wanted to do, but the look on Gloria's face said something about their relationship. Each time her sister had invited her to share time in her life, her world, her friends, she had always declined. It had never dawned on her that maybe her sister would take her rejection of her lifestyle as a rejection of her as a person.

Jennifer acquiesced. "Sure, what is a good time to come by and get in on the center of the finger snaps?

Gloria's was stunned. "Seriously? You're coming?"

"Sure, why not? It will be fun. Then I get to meet some of your friends and hang out in your world. Will your girl be there?"

Her jaw dropped. It was the only the second time in their lives that Jennifer had acknowledged she knew Gloria was gay. She watched Jennifer suspiciously, "Yeah. She will be there?"

"Great! I get to hear her opinion on that new recipe for those wings. I am thinking about serving those in my bistro." Jennifer looked at her watch. "Ooh, I don't want to be late for my date!" She hugged Gloria again and shimmied her shoulders before darting off to grab a shower.

Gloria was still standing in the kitchen. She grabbed the kitchen phone to check the caller ID. No calls from any doctor's office. No one was dying. Still. It felt weird. But it was a good weird.

She arrived at Tony's right at 6:15, wearing a red top, black slacks and a medium heel. Her hair was up since she didn't have time to style it, and she wore small, hooped earrings with just a touch of gloss on her lips. She felt sexy. The top wasn't too low, the pants weren't too tight and she felt good.

Nervous fingers pushed the doorbell as she waited for him to answer. And when he opened the door, her breath caught. He had a haircut, a shave and looked amazing in a fitted, light blue shirt, navy slacks with a shiny belt buckle and sharp looking navy dress shoes. He looked as good as puffed pastry filled with sweet meats and warm mousse. "Wow! You look amazing," she told him as she leaned forward to kiss his cheek.

Tony turned his head so that he could catch her lips instead. "So do you, Jennifer."

A large smile on her face, she extended her arm to him, asking if he was ready. Jennifer planned to sweep him off his feet tonight as she escorted him to her car and even opened the door for him. She was about to break every rule she had ever been taught, but tonight she didn't care. Her first marriage was a whisk off to Vegas and she had little say in how things went as she allowed her husband to make all the decisions in the relationship and it didn't turn out too well. This time around, she was going to start it out right. Plus, she was going to make her own damn decisions about what she wanted. She wanted this man.

Tony didn't know what to say about her opening the door for him or her giving him the armed escort, but it was her date, and he would go along with whatever she had in mind. As long as it was within reason. "I know a great little place to grab a bite to eat before the show," she said as she slowly backed out of the drive.

She was right. It was a little place. It was so tight he was afraid to raise his hand because he would knock out the person behind him with his elbow. The restaurant was little, but the prices weren't. Dinner for the two of them was equaled to his two-week food budget for him and Sasha.

"Jen, this is really pricey," he told her.

"Get whatever you want. I am taking you on the date. Remember?"

"I know, but this is pretty expensive," he told her.

She winked at him. "Yeah, since I'm dropping this kind of money, you may want to think about putting out later this evening. My backseat lets down. Now give mama some sugar with yo fine ass."

"Mama?"

"You know what it does to me when say it like that." She grinned as she replayed the words he had used on her the first night.

This opened the conversation between them. He talked about his business, and she spoke of hers. As the meal progressed, she learned a great deal about him and she was quick to share her thoughts as well.

They talked about personal finance. They talked about children, church, life, personal goals and dreams. She impressed herself by not saying what she thought he wanted to hear, but how she truly felt. He impressed her by being okay with it. She stopped talking and stared at him.

"What?" he asked.

"I dunno. I am so awed by you. I don't know what to

say or think," she said.

"This is who I am, Jen. I am a very honest man who lives a quiet life. I was in divinity school when I messed up and created Sasha, so I had to change my major. I don't regret it, because my daughter is amazing," he told her.

"You know God forgives, Tony," she told him.

"Yes, but parishioners do not. I had no intention of marrying Sasha's mother and I really wanted nothing to do with the woman," he said.

"May I ask what happened?"

"She wanted me and not the child. She set out to get me and I was not very skilled with women or wise, and she knew it. I was 19 and she was 18. She assumed we would get married and when I told her I had no intention of marrying her, she threatened to do away with my daughter. I would not hear of it, so I continued to see her throughout the pregnancy until she was past the point of termination, then I slowly backed away. When the delivery time came, I asked for the child. She agreed with the stipulation that she would not be a part of Sasha's life. With the help of my parents and my sister, we got through those first tough years. I managed to finish college and through the church picked up a few graphic jobs. I took some contract work so I could be home with her until she started kindergarten, and the rest is history."

Jennifer watched his face. She asked, "It has been lonely for you, hasn't it?"

"Yes, it has."

Now was her time to put it all out there. She wanted this man in her life. Actually, she wanted him for the rest of her life. "I would like to end your lonely days, Anthony Peay." She reached in her purse and pulled out an elongated black box and handed it to him.

"What's this?"

He opened it to find a man's bracelet inside. "This is really nice. You didn't have to buy me a present, Jen. I don't know what to say."

"Say yes."

Tony squinted his eyes as he looked at her. He wasn't sure what the question was. "Yes, I will accept the bracelet?"

She laughed. "No. I am asking to share your life. I am asking you to be mine. That is my engagement gift to you?"

He sat the bracelet down and stared at her. "Jennifer, did you just ask me to marry you?"

Oh Snap...

There are times in a man's life that can be considered moments that are burned in the memory. The birth of Tony's daughter was at the top of his list. The death of his father was also high on the charts, along with his mother's recent confession, but this ... Tony's mind was blown.

"I mean, not right away, of course, but once we ... you know ... make it formal and date some more ..." Jennifer was stuttering.

"Get over here with your fine ass," he said as he literally lifted her out of the chair and deposited her on his lap. Something which was no easy feat considering how tight the space was in the restaurant. "Of course I will marry you." He kissed her hard on the mouth as he nearly squeezed the life out her.

She kissed him back, then she pulled back to look in his eyes. "So your answer is yes?"

"Yes. Yes, a thousand times yes. I will marry you." Tony P was no one's fool, but he knew something was up.

As Jennifer settled the check and they climbed into her car. He stared at her in the dimly lit vehicle. He had to know. "So how bad is your family?"

"What do you mean?"

"You proposed to me the day before I am scheduled to meet them. How bad are they?"

She only grinned as she merged onto I-75 southbound. "Well I love them. Have you told your family about me?"

"Yes," he sighed.

"And?"

"And what? I'm happy and that is all that matters," he said to her as he slipped his fingers to interlace with the hand that wasn't holding the steering wheel. There was a *but* coming and she could feel it.

Jennifer wanted to know, "What is it?"

He didn't really know how to broach the subject but it needed to be addressed before anything went any further. "We will have to undergo six months of marriage counseling before we say the I do's. My church requires it. I hope you are okay with that?"

"I can handle that. My church requires something similar," she told him but there was something else he wasn't saying.

"Spill it, Tony P," she said as she pulled her hand away to signal and place both hands on the wheel.

"There is an abstinence period before the wedding as well," he said. That didn't bother Jennifer. Until Tony she had been abstinent for nearly 18 months.

"I can handle that as well, but can you?"

"Hell no. I want to pull over right now and make love to you," he said as he burst into laughter. "That scent of lavender and lemongrass that you are wearing is making me feel like some sort of rutting bull." It reminded him of the lemongrass he had thrown onto his sheets when he made love to her. He started to snort and shake his head.

She pulled into the parking lot of Gloria's building and Jennifer parked the car. Tony was no longer smiling as he eyed the brick structure and all the hipsters walking into it. *Trust. Trust the journey.* He slipped his hand into hers as they made their way to the door and Jennifer handed the attendant a twenty.

Inside the building, the room was dark. Candles were burning and everything smelled like patchouli and coconut oil. Tony was frowning as he looked at her. She had taken him to one of *those* poetry things where people yelled out angry words and others snapped their fingers like drunken hippies at a love fest. He was shaking his head no and walking towards the door, but was stopped by a very angry looking black woman with an Afro. She was an unusual looking woman with large, wide set eyes, an upturned pug nose and a little tight mouth that housed a really big set of oversized teeth.

The woman looked at Jennifer. "Is this him?" Her face held a scowl.

"Yes, this is Tony Peay. Tony this is my sister, Gloria," Jennifer said. It was a horrible moment as Tony's eyes went from Jennifer back to her sister. From her sister back to Jennifer. A look of confusion covering his expression.

Gloria asked, "What does the P stand for?"

He crinkled his nose. "My last name. My last name is Peay."

Gloria was now confused. "Pee, as in pee-pee?"

"No as in Peay. Peay. Like Austin Peay," Tony's face was contorted.

"Who or what is Austin Peay?" Gloria asked.

"The college," he said.

"You went to Austin Peay?"

"No! My last name is Peay. P-e-a-y? People just call me Tony P."

Gloria frowned at him, giving him a *whatever* look. "I saved you guys a table up front. And hey, your wings and meatballs were a big hit!"

They followed Gloria to their seats as they were seated next to a rather large busted woman who introduced herself as Katie Mae. Her long dreadlocks hung down between her massive breasts and Tony did his best to look everywhere but at the woman. Or those massive mammaries. His attempts failed after Gloria bent down to kiss her while juggling one of the oversized boobies.

"Dear Jesus," Tony said as he focused his stare at the stage.

Katie Mae jiggled the jugs at Gloria as she took to the dais to introduce the next poet. A little, runty, hostile woman who called herself Blood. She also had props that spewed red liquid as she yelled into the mic about the blood spilled by the white man. She kept looking at Tony.

Tony kept looking at Jennifer, who was staring at Katie Mae who was still fondling her boobies and looking at Gloria. Blood finished her piece by pretending to sever her carotid, which spewed more red liquid onto plastic covering on the stage. The whole thing was a mess. It took everything in Jennifer not to lose it when Tony leaned over and whispered in her ear, "I don't know who is angrier, Blood or your sister. They both are scary as hell. And I ain't no punk, but I am scared. Can we leave?"

Jennifer patted his thigh as she shook her head no. Tony poked out his bottom lip as he watched a young man with a chicken wing hanging out of his mouth run a mop across the stage. Gloria was back on the podium saying something about her sister the chef who provided the food. The dude on the stage waved the chicken wing at Jennifer and said thanks. The next act was up. Tony was still looking confused. He wanted to let Jennifer know that he didn't get out much and this was, well, too much. He watched the next act climb on stage.

This poetess was yelling, too.

So was the next one.

And the next.

They were all so angry.

The final act was a young man named Sleepy Jonz, and he came to the stage with a guitar. His words were melodic as he spoke from his soul about what it means to be a black man in America. Tony was enthralled. He leaned forward as he physically felt the power of the young man's words and was shocked when he felt the emotion welling up inside of himself. He related much of it to Raheem and some of the things he underwent. He thought about his brother Tino, and wondered if he had experienced any of this as well. Sleepy began to sing a chorus and then came back to his words. When he finished, Tony was astounded.

Gloria noticed and walked over and placed her arm around his shoulder. "Pretty powerful stuff, huh?"

"Yeah, it was. His lyrics touched me," he told her.

It was then that Gloria Taylor did something very people ever had witnessed – she smiled at Tony. "You are alright, Tony P. Are you by chance related to the Rev. Isaiah Peay?"

His eyebrows shot up. "Yes, he was my father."

"He was a good man, Tony. I had a chance to work with him on a few projects through my nonprofit for battered women. His church was our meeting place before we bought this building."

For the umpteenth time that evening, Tony was surprised. "You provide counseling for women?"

"I am an administrator, but I have contracted certified counselors who work with our clients," she told him over the roar of the crowd that was breaking up and people were vying for her attention. Gloria was very popular. People were calling her name, thanking her for a great evening. Several people thanked Jennifer for the food and asked for her business cards. This was the first time that Jennifer had seen her big sister in her element. She felt proud of Gloria as she watched her talk to Tony.

"I have a special case that I would like to discuss with you." He was a grateful now that he had come.

"Let's talk some more tomorrow after dinner," she said as she patted his arm and walked away. She told Jennifer she would see her tomorrow and thanked them both for coming. Who would have thought? Tony turned to look for Jennifer who appeared to be suffocating in Katie Mae's bosom as the woman held her too close for nearly too long.

Tony rescued her and pulled her out the door. The drive back to his house was quiet as he was still processing the idea that out of chance, Jennifer's sister would be the link to getting his mother some much needed help. He was grateful. Although he had prayed about it, he had not expected an answer so soon.

Tony stared at his lovely Jennifer. He had prayed for someone to share his life as well. The whole thing was surreal and he was completely dumfounded by his fortune. *I will take it all.*

It was sweet of Jennifer to walk him to the door. "I will text you my address tomorrow. We will look for you and Sasha around four. Dinner is at 5:30."

He didn't hear a word she said. He was too busy

staring at her mouth. Then he started to shake his head before she even asked the question.

"Tony, do you want me to come in?"

He was still shaking his head no. "If you come in, then some part of your body is going to end up in my mouth."

Jennifer stepped closer to him. "... Or, if I come in, some part of your body may end up in mine."

Tony began to fumble with his keys, trying to get the door opened, but as he reached for the lock, the door was opened by Sasha. "Hey, Daddy! Hey, Chef Jennifer!"

The disappointment that covered Tony's face was almost audible as he hugged his daughter. "I thought you were staying at Aunt Cleo's tonight?"

"Nope, she said I should be home when you got here. I also wanted to come home and surprise you. Are you surprised, Daddy?"

"Am I ever ..." he told her with a forced grin. Jennifer shielded her laughter.

"Plus, I wanted to see Chef Jennifer to ask what I should wear tomorrow," she said with a huge grin.

"Whatever you choose will be fine, Sasha," Jennifer said as she hugged the girl, giving her a kiss on her forehead and light one to Tony's lips. Then she left the porch, telling them both she would see them tomorrow.

20 Peace, be still...

It was a quiet Sunday morning as everyone filed into First Baptist Church. The first family took their seats in the second row as the Rev. Waldo Jones began his sermon. Normally, the sermons were dry and without any real heft and feel, but this Sunday, it was as if the pastor had been given a message to deliver. He started to speak on the importance of peace. The words resonated with Tony as he understood the meaning of the verses since he had met Jennifer. His sleep was peaceful, his workday was serene, and life had taken on a new meaning. His arm went around his mother's shoulders and she leaned into his strength. In the pastor's words was the formation of a power that Tony held up his left hand in the air to capture. He balled up his fist to hold onto the spirit in his hand because before he could become a great husband, he had to be a great son. It was time for his mother to find some amity, as well. It was his duty to weed the walk path so she could begin her journey.

After church, Cleo and her husband joined them at his mother's home for lunch. Waldo seldom came over unless it was a holiday or a special occasion. Today was. Today was going to be a day of healing. If there was ever a time when Tony was proud of his little sister, today was one of those days.

Over chicken salad sandwiches with green salad, she looked at her mother. "Momma, it's time for you to find some peace," she started the conversation. This was of course after Waldo had blessed the food and looked at the sparse spread with disdain. He had been expecting more, but their mother was not a big eater, neither were her children. To them, the meal was a bounty.

Jacqueline's eyes were clear as she looked at her daughter. "You know nothing about my pain! You have no idea what I have been through, so don't sit at my table and tell me how I should feel about my life!"

Cleo, normally, at this point would back down. Whenever their mother raised her voice, his sister would crumble and cave. But not today. With her back rigid and determination shrouding her face, she marched forward. "You're right. We don't, and we don't need to know the details. What we want and need you to know is that, as your children, we will love you and respect you as our mother, no matter what the circumstance."

The gaze was unflinching as Jacqueline's eyes went to Sasha. Tony saw no reason for her not to be at the table or to be a part of the process. If Jacqueline was to heal, it was going to take all of them to bring her back to a healthy place.

"You want to speak of this in front of him and her?" she asked as she looked at Waldo and then at Sasha.

"We are your family. Each of us stands beside you and behind you, Momma. We are here to help bear your load," Cleo said with firmness.

"You have no idea what cross I bear and what burdens I carry," their mother said through gritted teeth.

Cleo was still standing firm. "You are correct, Momma, and I don't. But this I do know. We could care less about how Tino was conceived, but you gave him life. You nurtured him and gestated a healthy newborn. He was given to and raised by relatives who loved him and from what I hear, raised him to be a very successful man."

Tears started to run down Jacqueline's cheeks and well-worn fingers swatted away the streams of salty memories. "I did check on him."

Tony spoke up. "Yes, you did. I went with you to his high school graduation and his graduation from college."

Cleo's eyes got wide. She never knew any of this. "Momma," she said as she watched her mother's face. "It's time to get to know him. He is not responsible for how he came into this world or for the actions that created him. He has thrived and prospered as a testament that God still favors you and He looked out for your son."

The tears were pouring down Jacqueline's face as her thin body wracked with tears. Sasha jumped up and held her grandmother tight. "It's okay, Nana. I met him and he is so nice. He is strong and handsome and he gave me this for my birthday." She showed her grandmother the necklace.

Cleo didn't know that part either. "Momma, Tino has found it in his heart to still want to love you and us as well. Turning him away again would be to tell God you don't want His blessing."

"I don't know if God will forgive me for what I have done," she said with her head held low as Sasha still held her tight.

Sasha spoke again. "He is a forgiving God, Nana. He will not forsake you if you do not forsake Him. He has probably been waiting for you to talk to Him about Uncle Tino for a long time."

Tony was outdone. His daughter was right. It took him years to regain his courage to ask for anything because he had fallen short and conceived a child out of wedlock. He had also forsaken divinity school out of fear of his own sins. He had not prayed for many years for himself until three months ago.

"Mom, are you ready to talk to Tino?" Tony asked.

Jacqueline nodded her head as Tony punched in the number and handed the phone to his mother. Tino answered on the third ring. "Tino Boehner." His voice cracked through the breath she had been holding.

She knew exactly what to say because she had been practicing the words for many years. "Valentino, this is Jacqueline, your mother."

It was the phone call Tino Boehner had been longing to receive for the majority of his life. This was his chance to be complete and fill the hole that rendered him empty. It may only be a spoonful of dirt, but it was a start.

Ebony was trying hard to make the spaghetti come out right, but she was a lousy cook. No matter how hard she tried, and even if she followed the directions to the letter, nothing ever came out right. Her mother banned her from the kitchen at her house and she sincerely was thinking of banning herself from her own kitchen. Tino looked at the plate of gooey pasta and shook his head no.

"I think we should go out," he said as he picked up the plate and took it to the kitchen. He scraped the pile of potential diarrhea in the sink and dumped the pot as well.

"That is just rude!" Ebony told him. "I worked so hard on that, trying to make you dinner, you big brute."

He started the garbage disposal and dumped the rest,

grinding and rinsing away any attempts to potentially kill him. "I know, sweetie, but it looked scary. Instead, let me take you out, or we order some Chinese or something." Ebony was pouting. As he reached for her, his phone rang. He held up a finger for her to wait a second while he took the call.

"Tino Boehner," he said in the phone as his finger ran over Ebony's bottom lip. He was not ready for what he was about to hear.

"Valentino, this is Jacqueline, your mother," she said with a voice that sounded like it was filled with emotion.

The look on his face concerned Ebony as she visibly saw Tino's legs go weak and he grabbed for the couch. "Hello, Jacqueline," he responded.

"I don't travel much anymore, but I would love to see you. If you are ready, I would like to meet your fiancée as well. Anthony tells me you are about to get married," she said into the line.

"Yes, Ma'am, I am." He was quiet for a second. "Jacqueline, I don't have any questions. I am not looking for any reasons why. I just want to get to know you and my family." He felt that portion was important.

"I understand," she told him. "And thank you."

"No, thank you for agreeing to see me," he said as he rubbed his hand across his chest. His heart felt as if it were about to burst.

"Valentino," she whispered into the phone. "I loved you enough to do right by you. Giving you to Tom and Mary was the right thing for you."

"They raised me well, Jacqueline," he paused for a second, putting together the words. The line was quiet. "Thank you for loving me enough to give me life."

Say Cheese...

"What do you think he is like, Daddy?" Sasha asked as she fidgeted in the seat while he followed the navigation on his phone to the address she had given. It was a very swanky neighborhood and both he and Sasha's mouth dropped when the GPS lead them to the drive of the house Jennifer called home. It was a mini mansion.

"Wow! Daddy, $500 an hour gets you this much house? I know I want to be a chef!" Sasha said.

Tony was a bit off put by what he was seeing. He had mentioned money over the cost of dinner last night, but he had no idea that she even had this sort of background. By the looks of things, Jennifer grew up in wealth. He had known the general area that she grew up in based on the school she had attended, but he had not expected any of this.

He rang the doorbell to be greeted by a middle aged Hispanic woman in a maid's dress. "I'll get the door, Vella," Jennifer said as she bounded down the stairs.

"Hey, guys, come on in," she said as casually as if asking if they wanted extra fries with their meal. He didn't know why it made him uncomfortable, but he was. In the back of his head, he was tamping down the resentment of feeling as if she had not been honest with him.

Sasha was not put off at all. "This is a great house, Chef Jennifer."

"Thanks, I grew up here. Come on in guys and meet my dad," she said as she led them past the formal living room with white furniture, the formal dining room with plush white furniture and into a gigantic great room with a walk in fireplace that fed into a dream kitchen. Sasha's mouth was wide open.

Johnny Taylor looked up from the counter where he was cutting up chicken breasts to take a look at his daughter's new guy. Never one to hold his tongue, he said what was on his mind. "You are white!"

Tony smiled at him. "Yes, sir. I have been all of my life."

He watched Jennifer's father wash his hands before he walked over to greet them both. Tony held his ground. "Mr. Taylor, this is my daughter, Sasha."

She extended her hand to shake his, and Johnny Taylor's tight lips peeled back to reveal a set of oversized teeth. Jennifer was right, Gloria looked just like their father. "Nice to meet you, Sasha. You can call me G-Pop," he said.

Jennifer's eyes rolled up in her head. "Good grief, Daddy, you just met them. How can you have her call you G-Pop?"

"She is the closest thing I have right now to a grandchild. A man has to start somewhere, especially since my daughters will not grace me with the beauty of having my own flesh and blood grandbabies. Sasha here will have to fulfill that need," he said with sadness in his eyes.

"Tony, can I get you something to drink? A soda or something?"

"No thank you, sir. I'm fine. Can I help with anything?"

Johnny turned to face his daughter's new man, "You

any good on the grill?"

"Yes, sir, what do you need me to do?"

"Head out on the patio and get it fired up so I can get this chicken on. Sasha, you come with G-Pop and help get the salad started, then Jennifer can show you the house," he told the child, who was happy to lend a hand.

"Yes, sir, G-Pop!" Sasha said with enthusiasm. *Great, she is fueling his fire.*

Tony stepped out onto the patio and he didn't know why he was shocked, but it wasn't a standard grill – it was an outdoor kitchen. He also could not take his eyes off the very large covered in ground pool. It was difficult to keep his focus when he really wanted to strip down and jump in the pool and swim a few laps. A private pool is so nice. When he was growing up, the only thing they had were summer camps the church sent them to where he would get to swim in the lake.

He worked diligently and soon the gas grill was nice and hot and he stood on the patio, hands in his pockets, taking in the peacefulness of the back yard and the meticulous landscaping. Johnny walked up silently and stood beside Tony, asking, "Nice, isn't it? I always imagined this yard filled with tons of kids and friends and family. I mean when they were growing up, there were plenty. As they grew into adult women, I hoped by now this yard would be full again with my grandkids."

"It is still early, Mr. Taylor," Tony told him as he gazed longingly at the pool. Before anything more could be said between them, Gloria arrived with Katie Mae and two hellions that made a beeline for the pool. The two boys stopped only long enough to remove their shoes before they dove into the water.

Johnny looked about like he was being invaded by the Japanese at Pearl Harbor. Sasha heard the kids and the splashing in the water and ran outside. "Whoa! G-Pop, you have a pool? Can I swim, Daddy? Can I get in?"

"You don't have a suit, sweetie," Tony told her as the two boys climbed out, ran around the pool and did a cannon ball into the water.

"There are some suits in the pool house," Johnny told him. "Just make sure that door is closed when you are in there changing, young lady."

"Yes, sir, G-Pop," Sasha said as she took off to the mid-sized building that was more like a small two-bedroom house and located a one-piece suit. Tony was watching his daughter and Johnny's eyes were focused on Katie Mae. Tony didn't need to turn around to know what his future father-in-law was staring at. The woman was wearing a low cut blouse over a bikini top.

"Daddy, this is Katie Mae. In the pool are her boys, Raja and Domini," Gloria said.

Poor Johnny had tried to keep his eyes upward. He even tried to focus on his daughter, but the pull of the eye to all of those boobies was too much for the old man. "Good Lawd, girl, you can feed an African Village with those things!"

Tony nearly choked. Gloria's mouth was wide but Katie Mae took it as a compliment and flung herself at Johnny, hitting him chest first with all those tatas. "Oh, Daddy, you are funny just like Gloria said. She told me you were a straight shooter."

"Why in the hell is she calling me Daddy, Gloria?" Johnny asked and Tony turned his back to stifle his laughter. "And who are these people?"

"Daddy this is my *friend*, Katie Mae," she arched her brows at him when she said friend.

Johnny was not looking at Tony, whose cheeks were flaming red as he tried to hold in the gut-busting laugh that was threatening to overtake him. He excused himself to go and get the chicken to place on the grill, but Johnny followed him inside.

"All I ask is to be put on the granddaddy playing field before I close my eyes and meet your dear mama in Heaven. Is that too much to ask?" Johnny said out loud to anyone who was listening although he was looking at Tony.

Jennifer was prepping the corn for the grill when she looked up at Tony. "Careful, he wants something."

Tony lowered his voice. "What makes you say that?"

"If you knew my mama, you'd know that woman was not in Heaven," Gloria whispered. She had come inside, as well, as Katie Mae dove into the pool with her sons.

"Tony," Johnny said as he picked up a football. Where it had come from was an entirely different question that Jennifer was not going to ask. Knowing her father as she did, he had purchased it especially for this moment. It was a prop. A visual speaking aid that was going to sell some point he was about to make. "I just want to get in the game. I want to be a granddad. Can you help an old man out, son?"

Tony inhaled deeply and expanded his chest, flexing his arms and doing deep knee bends. "If I'm put in the game, coach, I will give it the old college try." He pulled his knee up to his chest in a stretch.

"That's what I'm talking about, Tony! Commitment," he placed the football in his grip holding it out for a rallying cry. "On three, Tony, give me a go, fight, win, son," Johnny said as Tony gripped the football and in unison, the two counted to three and yelled out, "Go, Fight, Win!"

Jennifer was beyond done. "Can this day get any crazier?"

He heard a familiar sound from the pool and Johnny ran to the back door and began to yell at Domini and Raja. "You two get your hands off my grandbaby!" The boys were ganging up on Sasha in the pool and trying to hold her under water. Vella had gone out back to carry towels to the pool for the kids as she too was trying to stop the boys. Sasha was holding her own.

The doorbell rang as Gloria headed to the front door and Tony headed out the back to check on his daughter and the chicken on the grill. Katie Mae was floating on her back or her boobs were floating her, he was uncertain, but Tony tried not to stare, but he felt Gloria was a better man than him to tackle all that woman.

"Who's at the door, Gloria?" Jennifer yelled. Gloria rounded the corner with her cell phone camera ready pointing it at Jennifer.

"Well, who is it?" she asked again.

"Your husband. Say cheese," Gloria said as she snapped the expression on her little sister's face. At first, Jennifer thought she was kidding until she looked up and saw Michael standing in their kitchen.

His deep baritone filled the air. "Hello, Jennifer."

Love does not hurt...

It was a surreal moment as she stared at the man she had been married to for two years. He looked the same as he had when she handed him the divorce papers and moved into the guest room – blank. That was the thing about Michael. He was an actor, an empty slate waiting to be affixed with a purpose, or someone to yell at him, "action." It seemed the only way the man knew what to do or how to do anything was when he was taking on a role.

Still no words were formed as she stood behind the counter and eyed him with a curious stare. Now that she had something substantial to compare him with, Michael as a husband was coming up short. She had only known Tony for almost two months and felt closer to him than to this man that she had invested two and a half years of her life into. She didn't hate him. Instead, she felt a deep-seeded pity. He would never know what love was, because in his world, love hurts.

He had hurt her, sometimes intentionally, other times by acts of omission or attrition. His actions ate away at her self-confidence and her perception of herself as a woman. At one point, she actually believed it was her fault that he cheated because she was always too tired to fully give all of herself to him in bed. As she stared at him, a smile crept across her face along with the realization that truly, "It was not me, it was you." They were not a good match. He didn't see her and he could not feel her spirit. If you can't feel it, then you can't feed it.

Tony fed her. She could feel him and it was grand.

"I know this is a surprise, Jennifer, but are you at least going to say something more?" Michael asked her.

"Love doesn't hurt," she said as she grinned at him like the sun had just begun to shine after a month of rainy days.

"I know that now," he told her and moved towards where she was standing, but the back door opened and in walked Tony with a platter of grilled chicken. He was followed by a soaking wet Sasha and Raja, who had a nosebleed. Vella was trying to help, but Johnny had come into the kitchen and was helping the young boy, all the while fussing.

He looked up and saw Michael.

He saw him at the same time Sasha and Tony spotted him. Sasha squealed and ran over to ask for his autograph. It still had not connected with Tony, who the man was other than a famous actor as he walked over and extended his hand. "Micheal Ealing, hey, I'm Tony P." The two shook hands as the men stared at each other.

Michael's eyes went to Jennifer.

Jennifer's eyes stayed with Tony.

Tony's eyes went back and forth between the two and suddenly, he connected the pieces. "Oh! You are that Michael!'

Without missing a beat, he looked at Jennifer. "Is he staying for dinner? Sasha is about to set the table, we have room for one more, right?"

Jennifer asked the question. "Michael, would you care to join us for dinner?"

It was an odd moment as every eye in the room looked at him. Michael swallowed. "If it isn't an imposition?"

Tony was cool. "There is always room for one more." He turned his attention to his wet child. "Sasha, shower, change, and hurry so you can help G-Pop set the table."

Having had the tour of the house earlier, Sasha knew where Jennifer's room was and headed in that direction. But Johnny wasn't too happy with Tony inviting that man to stay. Michael must have sensed it. "Mr. Taylor, good to see you again."

Johnny only grunted, "How you doing Micheal?" He did not wait for an answer as he asked Tony to join him on the patio. "Tony, son, come help me shut down this grill." He added extra emphasis on the son.

Before the back door even closed, he lit into Tony. "Why the hell you asking that man to break bread at my table? I don't even like that son of a booger and I want to know why he is in my house?"

Tony, calm and composed answered, "Sir, he is part of her history. I am her future. He needs to see for himself that she has moved on so he can as well."

Johnny stood still staring at Tony. "Gloria said you are Isaiah Peay's son."

"I am. You knew my father?" he asked.

"Yes, we worked with him to set up Gloria's nonprofit. Your dad was a good man," he said to Tony. "You seem to be a lot like him."

"I can only hope to be worthy enough in your eyes for you to accept me as your son-in-law. I would like to ask you for Jennifer's hand in marriage," Tony said firmly as he looked back in the window at her.

"Tony, I would be pleased to have you and Sasha in my family," he told him as he turned off the gas on the grill. He mumbled under his breath as Katie Mae dragged herself out of the pool. "Well, let's go inside and get this circus moving." He called to the boys and Katie Mae to get cleaned up for dinner.

He only shook his head as the woman and her breasts made their way towards the house. "Good Lawd, save me from the choices of my children," Johnny mumbled under his breath.

Dinner progressed amazingly well considering Katie Mae's children occupied most of the conversation with bad jokes, arguing amongst themselves and in between mouthfuls of chicken and corn on the cob, yelled at Jennifer, "This is some good grub." Katie Mae sat making googly eyes at Gloria, who was truly embarrassed in front of their father.

Johnny called her out on it. "Why you acting all embarrassed now? She acts the same way when you are around your friends. The woman seems to be in love with you, Gloria." He whispered it so the kids could not hear it.

Domini wanted to know. "Mr. Taylor, can we call you G-Pop, too?"

"Why? You planning to be around a lot?" Tony bit his lip to keep from laughing.

Raja answered for his brother. "Yes, sir! I can help with chores, too, if you let us come and use your pool on the weekend. Domini can cut grass, too!"

"Oh, he can, can he?"

"Yes, sir. And I want to be a lawyer like you so we can

have a big fancy house like this, too," Domini said with pride.

Jennifer sat watching her father and she felt like a kid again during the Christmas holiday season, her absolute favorite time of year. Especially when it came to seasonal shows. She always considered her father to be a bit of a cross between Yukon Cornelius and the Grinch. Here he sat, in the middle of an island of misfit toys, Sasha on one side and Raja and Domini on the other, her grandchild-less father gained 3 grandchildren in one afternoon. She found herself smiling as Sasha grilled Michael about his choice of movie roles, all the while taking selfies with him in between bites of food. Gloria chatted with Tony about his mother and her needs and it was the most oddball and wonderful family moment their house had experienced in many years. The dining room table had not been full of family or laughter in countless seasons and Jennifer was struck by a superfluity of emotions that bubbled up inside and started to run down her face in liquid form.

Tony noticed immediately and gathered her in his arms. "Are you okay, Jen?"

She leaned into the power of his embrace. "Yes. It's just been so many years since this house has been so full of life."

All eyes were on them but Tony didn't care. "In a little while, we will be filling our home with sisters and brothers for Sasha."

"I know, Tony, I'm just being silly," she said as he planted kisses against her forehead.

"No, you're not. It's a nice feeling. I rather like it myself," he told her softly in her ear. It was now Jennifer's turn.

"Kiss me and tell me you love me, Tony," she said into the side of his neck.

His fingers wiped away her tears as he stared into her eyes. "I am so lucky. You are absolutely an amazing woman. I love you, Jennifer." The kiss he planted on her was to ensure that Michael knew her life had no room for him. The tender moment was ruined by Sasha, who had to add her two cents.

"You two need to stop, Daddy," she said in a matter-of-fact tone. "G-Pop, I came home from school and I found them trying to make me a little brother! It was gross!"

It was all that Michael needed to see. After dinner, he left the envelope he had brought for Jennifer on the kitchen counter. If she had any questions of him, she knew how to reach him. His chances of winning his wife back were long gone. She loved another man and had a family.

23

Fruit and fiber...

Tony walked around his house wearing lounge pants and a confounded expression after he saw Sasha off to school. Last night was odd, yet satisfying. Jennifer's father was a straight shooter and a smart man. He accepted Sasha as his grandchild, as well as Raja and Domini and by the end of the evening, even Tony found himself calling the man G-Pop. What really perplexed him was Michael. He never revealed why he was there or what he wanted.

Johnny commented on how cool Tony was being, and in truth, he had handled himself well. He saw no need for childish antics or a jealous temper tantrum, especially not in front of his daughter. Or Jen, for that matter. She had made her choice and chose him. Michael did not feel like a threat and therefore he saw no need to treat him like one.

What was threatening him was his desire for his Jennifer. In his heart he knew he could not last a whole year. Morally, he could not continue to sleep with her either, whether an engagement ring was on her finger or not. If she was going to be his wife, it had better happen soon, because he did not want to spend another day without them under the same roof and in the same bed. He needed to talk to her.

Tony reached for his phone to call his girl. He chuckled at the reference to his dad often used to describe his mother, and swiped the screen. The phone began to vibrate in his hand. Jennifer's face covered the screen.

"I was just thinking about you," he said as he answered the phone.

"I was thinking about you, as well," she replied. "Has Sasha left for school?" she asked.

"Yes, I was about to hit the shower, get dressed, and knock out some work before calling to see if I could take you to lunch," he told her as he leaned against the back of the couch.

Jennifer was grinning at his thoughtfulness, but she was a step ahead of him. "Why don't you get off the couch, take off those blue loungers and let me join you in the shower to wash your back?"

Tony jumped and began to look around as he spotted her on the front porch, peeking in the window. "Well, this is a pleasant surprise," he said as he opened the door and pulled her into his arms. "I was just thinking about you," he said to the top of her head. Jennifer pulled away from him to lock the front door and kick off her shoes.

"I hope you are thinking what I am thinking," she said as she began to discard clothing and make a beeline for his bedroom.

"Well, I am now," he replied as he followed her down the hall.

"Don't forget to lock the door!" she told him as she stripped down to her white tee and disappeared into the master bath, starting the hot water.

Tony's mind was all over the place, but his feet had remained affixed to the floor. He really needed a heart-to-heart with her. There were things he needed to say. He was about to ask her to wait until he stepped around the doorjamb and saw her perfect naked bottom poking out as she leaned to test the temperature of the water. All reason left him. He stripped down and lifted her into the shower with him, using his oversized sponge to soap, wash and enjoy the beauty of her feminine form. He kissed her everywhere his mouth could reach and places where the shower head would not forcibly drown him before turning off the taps and roughly drying them both.

He needed a bed to take care of the rest. Tony took his time as he made love to her unhurriedly, bringing them both to the peak of pleasure, and riding the wave in slowly. She felt so amazing and they were good together, but this could not continue. He had to put a stop to it.

"Jennifer, I need to marry you," he said to her. She was laying lazily half atop him, with her thigh draped across his, her calf rubbing against the fine hairs on his legs.

"We have already established that," she told him as her fingers toyed with the hairs on his chest.

"No, sweetheart. I need to marry you soon. Like in the next month or so," he told her as he looked down at her face.

"Why the rush? Are you pregnant?" She was laughing, but when she raised her head and looked at him, he was not smiling. "What's wrong, Tony?"

"I don't do this, Jennifer. And I definitely can't see us doing this for a whole year.... I mean, I thought maybe we could get past the 6 months, then get married, but that doesn't work for me, either... sneaking over while Sasha isn't here..." he went quiet.

"Jennifer, in twelve years, I have never done this and I am not about to start. I didn't want you sneaking in and out of my house like we're doing something wrong. And it feels wrong to me. I can't lie. I love you with every fiber of my being and I want to marry you," he said flatly.

"I love you, too, Tony, but..." she said as she gathered her thoughts, "... we have only been seeing each other for two months. And to get married... just like that?"

"Do you plan to keep looking for a husband and another man to be the father of your children?"

She sat up in the bed. "No, of course not."

"So I'm it, then? I am the one you have chosen?"

"Yes, of course."

"Then why wait?"

He had a point. She clutched the sheets to cover her breasts as she looked down at him, sprawled out on the bed. "You sure about this?"

"I can't be any more certain. I want to go to bed at night with you and wake up next to you in the morning. I want to have evenings at home watching Jeopardy and baking cookies. I am ready for us to be a family," he told her.

There was still some hesitancy in her gaze. He sat up, as well. "We will never know everything about each other and we have a great deal to learn, but that is part of the beauty of this. It will be done together."

"I'm in, but there are a lot of details we have to iron out in the next month or so," she told him.

His eyebrows were up. "Details like what?"

She exhaled softly. "I got an offer today on the Pretentious Puss. Someone wants to buy it and God knows I want to sell it. That place is sucking the life out of me.... And living arrangements, we have to discuss living arrangements."

"What's the big deal? We get married and you move in here with me and Sasha," he told her. To Tony it was a no brainer.

"I have a house, Tony," she said in a lowered tone.

"You stay with your dad."

"Yes, but the house is mine. My mother left it to Gloria and me. I bought Gloria out so she could buy the building we went to on Saturday night," she admitted.

"That is your house?" he said with total surprise.

"My grandmother left it to my mother and she and Dad added the pool house and updated it, along with the kitchen, but yes, it is my house," she told him.

This added a glitch that he was not prepared to handle, and he had an idea that popped into his head that he needed answered. "Out of curiosity, what did Michael want?"

She gulped hard. "He sold our house in Los Angeles and he was bringing me my half of the proceeds."

Tony was still sitting in the middle of the bed staring at her. To him, this was something very important and he needed her to understand before they moved forward. "Jennifer, my father was a preacher, like his father before him. I am not talking about the type of ministers with two cars and a private plane. They had a base salary and ministering to the congregation was their full time job."

It was clear she didn't understand, but he needed her to. "Material things don't mean much to me. What matters to me is family and love."

"I can give you those things," she said as she moved closer to him in the bed.

"Well, let's set a date, because I sure want to give you lots of love and add to our family," he told her as he pulled her back into the bed. "I want a son, Jen," he said to her as his mouth found hers. To him, this was just the fruit on the pound cake. Jennifer was going to be his wife, but first she had to survive dealing with his mother.

Pudding and more...

It was a quiet Saturday afternoon when Tino pulled up to his house. Since Jennifer was off last Saturday, she was not able to join them tonight. She did promise to come to the house tomorrow to meet his mother, and hopefully his brother, if Tino was still in town. It also depended on how well the get together went today. He had faith that all would go well and that their mother could have the conversation with her son so she could begin to heal.

It would also be a healing time for Tino.

Tony could not imagine growing up knowing he was adopted and not knowing who his parents were. The first thing that came to mind when she said Tino's father was a black man was the famous father figure actor that was being outed as the roofie rapist. He shook the idea out of his head. His mother wouldn't have an opportunity to be around someone of his fame during that time. In his heart, although he was a forgiving man, it was good that he did not know who hurt her, because he would go after the bastard. After speaking with Gloria over dinner, he was even more disheartened when she gave him the staggering number of women who had, in their lifetime, either been assaulted or violated by some man. Sometimes the men were strangers, but more often than not, the attacks were perpetrated by someone they knew. It had crossed his mind that Tino's father may have been someone his mother had known. The anger was welling up inside him again.

Right on time, Tino arrived and pulled into the driveway. Sasha was ecstatic and wearing the necklace her uncle had given her. Tony was surprised when a carmel skinned black woman got out of the car as well. He smiled at them both, welcoming each of them into his home.

"Hey, Uncle Tino," Sasha said as she threw her thin, muscular body into his arms. Her eyes went to Ebony. "Is this your wife?"

Tino was pulled into her enthusiasm. "Not yet, but soon. This is Ebony Miller." It was then that Tony realized that his daughter really needed a woman's touch as she opened her mouth, he began to pray for her to lose her voice.

"You are so pretty. You have pretty dark skin like G-Pop! I can't wait for you to meet him and Chef Jennifer, who is going to be my stepmom. I guess when you and Uncle Tino start having little pretty cream colored babies, and my daddy and Jennifer have pretty creamy colored babies, it will be like our own little diversity club. I think Chef Jennifer's sister, Gloria, is *a gay*. Ooh, ooh and then there is Raja and Domini ... those two are a trip. They are always all turnt up," she said with an OMG look on her face.

Ebony's mouth was wide open. Tino was laughing and Tony ... well, he wanted a light ray to shine on her vocal chords and seize them up.

"Sasha, will you get some drinks for our guests?"

"Sure, Daddy, I made strawberry lemonade like Chef Jennifer makes. You two aren't allergic to berries are you?" Ebony, still in awe of the 13-year-old, simply stared at the child.

"Ebony," Tony said. "Please don't be surprised by my child. I have been a single father and did the best I could," he said with a bit of embarrassment. "Besides, I need to school you on Cleo, Mom and Waldo before they get here so you two don't have any more shockers register to your face."

Tino took a seat and looked around the house. There was nothing fancy about any of the décor. It was rather plain, with a few pieces that may have been worth a few hundred dollars. His brother was either strapped for funds or lived a very humble life. It did not escape Tony's notice.

"My father was a minister. So were his father and his father before him. I only buy what I need and place very little value on the material," he said flatly.

It was the perfect segue for Tino, who asked, "Did she ever mention my father? Or who he could be?"

Tony clenched his fist, then relaxed his hand. "She has provided little, almost no information about him other than he was black."

Tino's mouth dropped and Ebony's eyes went to his crotch as she mumbled, "Well, that explains that...."

Tony watched his brother who was now standing and pacing. He was moving so fast that Ebony had to grab him to prevent him, knocking over Sasha when she returned with the lemonades. Tony asked, "Tino, are you okay?"

Suddenly, Tino stopped pacing, "No, I am not okay. I just found out that I'm black. That is not something you tell someone like, "Hey man, how about a beer?" Also did you know you were black?"

Ebony's feathers were ruffled. "You have a problem

with being black, Tino?"

He shook his head. "No, that is not what I meant. I mean, how would you feel? Seriously, the first thing that popped into my head was the slip you a Mickey dude...."

Tony busted up in laughter. "When she told me, I thought the same thing!"

It was uncertain why the two of them were trying to best each other with the famous man impersonations, sticking to old pudding ads. Ebony could not believe either of them. She cut through the silliness. "Tony, did she say or mention the relationship between her and Tino's father?"

The laughter ceased. "No, and we will never question her about it, you understand me? This is very troubling for her and we are getting her some counseling to help her deal with a number of issues. Giving away her child is at the top of that list."

His voice was stern as he continued. "However, from my understanding, when my father left to do his missionary work in Grenada is when you were born. It fits the timeline. She kept and raised you until he was due to return and that is when she sent you to live with Tom and Mary. I'm not sure if my father ever knew about you."

"So I was a dirty little secret?" Tino asked with a frown on his face.

Tony shook his head. "We," he said as he used his hand to make a circle which included the four of them, Sasha as well, "... have no idea about the grounds or the means of your conception. I will say this, when she mentioned your father was black, she retreated into herself to a very dark place."

Tino's eyes met him. "Are you saying I'm the product of rape?"

Tony shook his head fervently. "No! I said we have no idea what the circumstances are of your conception and we will never know unless she chooses to disclose that to you. It is not our place to know."

Tino was hit with a spark of anger, puffing up his chest to his big brother. "What do you mean? I have every right to know!"

Tony moved so fast that both Sasha and Ebony jumped. He stood toe-to-toe with Tino. "You wanted to spend some time with our mother and get to know her. Those were the terms. Be grateful for the blessing of life that she gave you and the blessing of a good family and a good upbringing. Understand?"

Tino backed down. "Yeah, I guess."

Tony did not back down at all. "Don't guess! Know! She could have aborted you, but she didn't. She checked on you and was there for the major events in your life. Regardless of how you were created or the circumstances which brought you into this world, Tino, she loved you enough to do those things."

It was not satisfactory enough for Tino, who felt he was still owed some form of explanation. Tony was going to smooth him over and give him one of the answers he needed. "Tino, I grew up in the house with her and I received no more love than you did, and she was married to our father."

Sasha worked hard on the late lunch, serving salmon with jasmine rice and bacon wrapped asparagus. Ebony could not get over that a 13-year-old could cook better than she could, and Tino would not let it go either. He asked Sasha to come up during the summer to provide Ebony some lessons. Although he had tried to convince Jennifer to come up as well, both turned him down.

Sasha was more direct. "Uncle Tino, cooking has to be a passion for you. The food has to speak to you, and if not, then you will not be able to cook." Ebony understood what she meant. Food to her was fuel. She ate enough to keep her belly from rumbling, but a bowl of soup and grilled cheese sandwich was enough for her. Yet, judging by the way Tino ate, she also understood that she must learn to cook. Another blessing that arrived with lunch was that the food was so good, no one was talking.

Jacqueline arrived right at four p.m., wearing a pink dress that she had taken pleasure in making this week. She made it special for the occasion. Her one piece of jewelry that was of value, the pearls given to her when her mother passed, hung about her neck. Nervous fingers toyed with the orbs as she stepped through the door and saw her son standing before her.

"Sasha you were right. Valentino, you are so handsome," she said as she opened her arms for him to come in for a hug.

Cleo and Waldo stood behind her and watched the warm reunion. When Tino finally extricated himself, he was able to meet his sister. "Hello, you," he told her, not sure what her reaction was going to be.

With Tino standing next to Tony, she could see the resemblance between her brothers, both favoring their mother, whereas she looked like Isaiah Peay had spit her out. "Valentino, this is my husband, the Reverend Doctor Waldo Jones."

Tino caught it right away. "So your name is Cleopatra Jones?"

"We have never seen the movie so don't ask. Sasha, what's for lunch?" she said as she stepped around her brothers to go lend a hand in the kitchen.

Waldo extended his hand for greeting as Tino's eyes went to Tony who quickly stated, "Let's have prayer and lunch."

It was a pleasant affair with no one knowing quite what to say to the other members at the table until Jacqueline broke the silence. "Valentino, if you had not stumbled into house flipping and real estate, what would you have wanted to do with your life?"

He smiled at his mother. "Believe it or not, I would have wanted to be a singer. I love jazz."

The smile that lit up her face was something neither Cleo nor Tony had ever seen from their mother. "Really? Me, too. I was going to be a jazz singer. I used to sing all the time in the traveling choir. Music was everything to me ..." her voice trailed off.

Ebony spoke up, "Well he inherited that part fair and square from you. I kid you not the man has a soundtrack for every moment of his life."

Tino frowned at her, directing his attention back to his birth mother. "Jacqueline, might I ask, what is one of your favorite songs?"

"Oh, it's been so long since I sang anything, Valentino, but I was always very fond of the Eagles," she said as she pressed her fingers to her lips. The crow's feet at the corners of her eyes gathered as she recalled a fond memory. Tino pulled his phone from his pocket and cued up *Love Will Keep Us Alive*. He took the first verses in a very clear tenor, which seemed to transfix everyone at the table. As he rounded the first section of lyrics, heading to the refrain as the music played, Jacqueline chimed in with a beautiful soprano voice, clear with perfect pitch, creating a beautiful harmony along with her son. The words took on new meaning for them both as she touched his hands, emphasizing the words *I would die for you*, with her fingers moving to his face. Tino fell apart, choking on the words he was trying to sing. Ebony lowered her eyes as they filled with tears watching the beautiful moment between mother and son.

Jacqueline held her son in her arms. "Just because I could not keep you, did not mean I didn't love you. You were a wonderful baby. So full of love. I could not help but love you. It broke my heart to give you away."

It was all he needed to hear. The details of his conception and his father became irrelevant. Tom Boehner was the only father he knew and the only one he needed to know. He also had two mothers. Both of whom loved him and gave him a life. Finally, the journey to understanding who and where he had come from was answered. He was no longer hungry for the knowledge and his appetite for understanding why she would give him away and keep the two other children did not matter to him. The hole was being filled, even if it was a pudding spoon, adding one serving at a time.

Ice Cream...

Jennifer was nervous as she walked up to the front door of the traditional colonial home with the oversized front porch. She loved the six rocking chairs and the pots of colorful flowers. The hummingbirds flitted around the feeder in the corner and the small table held a copy of a well-worn magazine. There was even a ring in the wood of the table where a glass sat frequently, possibly holding a refreshing glass of lemonade or ice tea on hot Southern evenings. This was where his mother loved to spend her time. The chair nearest the table also held a cushion that showed off the butt print of a thin woman who made this her spot of respite.

In her right hand she had brought along a bouquet of fresh flowers for her mother-in-law to be and her left hand held a very large bowl of her venison meatballs in a honey mustard barbeque sauce. It had taken her years to get the recipe just right, as well as figure out how to cook all the venison her dad would bring home each year. Even to this day, the home freezer was full of the stuff. She only hoped that Tony's family would like what she decided to bring.

Before she could ring the doorbell, she looked up to find Sasha standing in the old-fashioned screen door. "Oh! You startled me," Jennifer told the girl who was still watching her with some concern. "Is everything okay, Sasha?"

The door must have held a traditional fence gate latch,

which was released as the girl stepped out on the porch. "Yes, Chef Jennifer, but I was hoping we could have a word before you went inside to meet my grandma."

"Hmm ... sure," Jennifer told her as she stepped aside to allow the teen to pass. Sasha pointed at the chair for them both to take a seat.

She was like a little old lady trapped in a teenager's body. Sometimes she acted twice her age and others, she acted half of it. She was definitely an enigma that Jennifer had to learn to how understand and respond. "Our lives are about to change drastically, Chef Jennifer, and I felt it would be good for you and me to work out a couple of things before you marry my dad."

Jennifer didn't know what to say. What could she say? "Okay, what is on your mind?" The tone of her words made Jennifer nervous.

Sasha inhaled and exhaled as if she were about to deliver a boatload of bad news. "I don't really know how to say this or even how to ask this question, honestly..."

Jennifer leaned back in the rocker and crossed her legs. If they were going to have any type of relationship, Sasha had to feel comfortable to speak to her about anything, even if the discomfort was on her part. She would not rush her or assume she knew what was on the girl's mind. Closing her eyes, she leaned back in the chair and smiled.

It must have given the child confidence to continue what she needed to say. "I was just wondering, I mean ... you and my dad are going to be married ... and we are all going to be living together...."

Jennifer rolled her head to the left, opening her eyes to look at Sasha, but still said nothing. "I mean ... I can't go on calling you Chef Jennifer.... And calling you by your first name isn't proper...."

"What would you like to call me, Sasha?"

"I don't know! That's why I am asking you! What are you comfortable with? What do you want *me* to call *you*?"

It was a good and valid question that Jennifer had no answer to and she also did not feel like trying to find an answer right now. "We don't have to know right away. As we move forward as a family, we will play around with some monikers and see which one feels best for you."

"I mean at some point, if I feel comfortable enough, I would like to call you some version of Mom. Would that be okay?"

Jennifer gave her a full on grin. "I would love that, but only when you're ready. Anytime you are ready to call me Mom, I will be honored."

Sasha Peay was ready now. She had never had a mother or knew what it felt like to live under the same roof with one. Anxious was not a word she used often, but the whole scenario made her anxious. It would be nice, though, to come home from school and yell, *Mom, I'm home.*

She was also happy to admit that she was anxious for her new life to start as a whole family, with a dad, a mom and possibly a new little brother or sister. She would also have access to a pool. Summers were going to be grand.

Where is she? Tony was getting impatient, or Jennifer must have been running late. He could not stop pacing until Tino finally walked over to him. "Maybe you should wait for her on the porch."

He could only provide a small grin because he felt like a fool. *Why am I nervous?* Ideas zinged about in his head that he had only, twice in his life, brought a woman home to meet his mother. Once in high school, and she turned out to be psychotic. The second turned out to be pregnant. He frowned as he walked over to the screen door to let himself outside. *Maybe I am freaking out because I don't have a great track record with women.* Jennifer was the right woman. He knew it. He felt it in every essence of his being and when he reached the front door, he was able to see it for himself.

Standing on the porch was his future wife in a warm embrace with his daughter. He overheard the tail end of the conversation. Jennifer was consenting to let Sasha call her Mom. It nearly buckled his knees. He backed away from the door slowly and retreated to his childhood bedroom.

The squeaky old bed was still there, which complained audibly when he placed his weight on the side. He lowered his head, his elbows resting on his knees, and took a deep breath. In the privacy of his room, he shifted his position to the floor, where he took to his knees and began to give thanks.

Lunch was a very somber affair and oddly enough, Cleo took an immediate liking to Jennifer, although she had very little to say to Ebony. Ever the diplomat, Jennifer whispered to Ebony in the kitchen, "It's probably because I will be taking Sasha off of her hands."

"Yes, I met her yesterday and you are going to have your hands full," Ebony confided in her.

"Nah. I think she just needs some girl time, full time, you know what I mean?" Jennifer responded and was surprised when Jacqueline also answered.

"I agree with you, Jennifer. A mother is very important for the development of a young girl. She sees me as too old and her Aunt Cleo as too stodgy, but she relates to you," Jacqueline said quietly. "My Anthony is a lucky man to have you, Jennifer."

This statement, too, ruffled Ebony's feather's a bit, but it was remedied. "Ebony, I don't know Tino well enough to make a call on what he was like before you two became involved. However, I will ask this of you," she paused for a second. "You will need to learn to cook. He has made several comments about it, and that seems like something that is important to him."

"Mrs. Peay, he was a brute before we started dating. Now, he is still a brute, just a bit tender in his touch," she told his mother.

Jacqueline, dressed in a blue cotton dress, looked tired. "You two seem like very nice girls. I am really looking forward to some more grandbabies."

Ebony's eyes were wide while she mumbled, *no time soon*. And Jennifer placed her hands on her stomach hoping for the opposite. Like her father had reminded her, she was in her 30s. She didn't have a lot of time left.

She watched Tony washing the dishes with Sasha and admired his commitment to his daughter. In her heart, she knew she had chosen well. Tony Peay was like a cool scoop of vanilla ice cream on a hot Southern day. Now to get into the details needed before they could start a life together as a family.

Nuts...

Life, like love, can be a splendored affair, full of hopes and desires to begin a life with family, friends and common goals. The life Johnny Taylor had led was a quiet life that centered on his daughters and his wife. It had been a good life, full of promise and hope, until cervical cancer knocked on their doorstep. The pool house had just been built and the new patio constructed so that when summer rolled around, they would be ready to host pool parties for their girls. Gloria was 13 and Jennifer was about to turn 11.

The cancer not only stole Carlisa Taylor's strength, it also took her joy and any pleasantness that was left in their lives. She became a bitter woman, full of anger and resentment that Johnny would be alive and healthy, and she would no longer exist. She looked at her two daughters, Gloria, who looked so much like her father, and Jennifer, who looked too much like her. Gloria, like her father, tried to be optimistic, but Carlisa was dying. At 34 years of age, she was dying. The women were flocking about her house like vultures, picking over her things and trying to take her family. The sheer venom she spewed at anyone who came near her relegated her visitors to only her father, an aunt and the pastor, who, too, eventually stopped coming by.

Yet Johnny stayed at her side. He never spoke a harsh word to her until one day, when even he'd had enough of her histrionics and hatred yelled at her, "Would you just die already!"

He resented those words for the rest of his life. Somewhere in the middle of the night, Carlisa found enough strength to down the bottle of pain pills, which stole her last breaths in the wee hours of the morning. He knew because when he checked on her, the body was still warm. Johnny had not realized how tired he had been until after her form was taken from the house that he lay down and slept for nearly 16 hours. It had taken the cancer nearly three years to claim her, but it had claimed all of them.

Gloria, now 16, came out to her father as a proud lover of women and an advocated for women's rights. She graduated high school and went to a local women's college, where Johnny swore, she perfected her lesbianism. His beautiful 13-year-old Jennifer was his world and he doted on her. They were more friends than father and daughter, and she, too, eventually left the nest. No words could describe his joy when the baby bird came home. Now, as he had hoped, she found herself a nice man and was about to be married. Joy was coming back into the house again. It would be welcomed.

"You are in deep thought this morning, Daddy," Jennifer said.

He flipped the page of the paper. It was Wednesday. He had an early tee time today. "Yeah, I am headed out to the links in a few." His eyes were now on her. "What are your plans today?"

"Not sure yet. I was thinking of maybe heading to Tony's and having dinner with him and Sasha tonight," she said in a low tone.

"You can cook dinner and have them over here, it is your house," he told her as he looked over the rims of his glasses.

"I know, Daddy...."

"When you get married, they are moving in here right?"

Ah nuts! She wasn't prepared to have this conversation now. He knew it, but Johnny was ready for the conversation, therefore they were going to have it.

"We are planning to discuss it today actually, Daddy. Tony wants to move up the wedding date. He wants to get married right away versus later in the year," she said.

Johnny's face lit up. "Why, are you expecting something to change real soon?"

It took her a second to understand what he meant, but her father was hoping she was pregnant. *What is wrong with this picture?*

"No, Daddy, I am not expecting. Tony is just a bit old-fashioned and he doesn't feel comfortable with us ... you know ... um ... he wants us to be a family and live under one roof," she said.

He stood up to get himself another cup of coffee. "Just don't rush into another marriage unless you are ready, Jenny."

"I'm not young and lonely like I was in LA. Michael was slick and clever and he used me to get what he wanted. Tony and I want the same things," he said.

"Even so, I am still going to have him sign a prenup. The bulk of your assets, we will move to a trust for your children so he will not have access to any of your funds," he told her with a calm determination.

"That's fine, Daddy, but Tony isn't about material possessions. After meeting his family, I am convinced that he simply wants someone to love. His mother was a bit of a cold fish, so I doubt she was the type to pass out loads of kisses and praise. His sister is married to the minister of their church, and she, too, is an odd duck with no kids. Poor Sasha just wants a mom and someone to guide her and show her the way to womanhood," she confided.

"Are you ready to be her mother, Jenny? Are you looking forward to it?"

Jennifer poured herself a cup of coffee. "I am ready for my own family and, yes, I am. I look forward to helping her grow into the woman she wants to be. I look forward to sharing my life with them both." She saw the sadness in her father's eyes.

"I am sorry, Daddy," she told him.

"Sorry for what, pumpkin?"

"That I got in the way of you finding someone to share your life with, that I came in between you finding a new wife. I know I ran off a lot of women ..."

Johnny was laughing. "Some of those women needed to be run off!" He walked over and touched her cheek. "I am a grown ass man, you never stopped me from doing anything. I never remarried because I didn't want to. I never brought women into this house because it was disrespectful and technically, not my house."

She squeezed him tightly. "This is our home. You paid the bills, the taxes, the remodels ... it's your house, too."

"Legally, my name is not on it and it belongs solely to you. Once you marry and Tony and Sasha are ready to move in, I will move out," he told her.

Jennifer was taken aback. "Move out to where? You have lived in this house for nearly 40 years. Stop being ridiculous!"

"I am handing you over to your husband and you will

reside under his roof, under his care. I don't need to live under the same roof as you begin your life as man and wife," he told her.

Then he grinned really wide. "I am moving into the pool house. I had it remodeled last year."

Johnny Taylor. Her father. He was a great man and him living in the pool house was okay with her. Tony would have to be okay with it, as well.

Petit Fours...

It was a quiet Wednesday morning when Tony arrived to take a good look at the house. It was going to be his new home and some adjustments would need to be made before he and Sasha moved in, but in general, Jennifer was looking forward to sharing with him some decisions she was thinking of making. *I have to discuss this with my husband. My husband. Holy Toledo! I am going to be married! Again.*

There were so many things she wanted to discuss with him today, but her main concern was that they get through the morning and remained dressed. When the doorbell rang, she felt like it was prom night and her date had arrived.

"Good morning, beautiful," he said as he lifted her in his arms and kissed her with everything he had. He gave her the kind of kiss a sailor gives his woman when he returns from sea after six months of duty. Jennifer held on tight as her fingers tugged at his hair and she returned his affection.

"Good to see you, too," she told him as he put her feet back on the floor.

"Come, let me show you the whole house, share with you some ideas I was thinking about to make this our home and get some feedback from you on your ideas," she told him.

His eyebrows went up as they headed towards the kitchen, which she said was in great shape and required no work. There was a small office off the mudroom, which the housekeeper used. "Currently, she comes by three times a week. I'm probably going to reduce that to once a week," she told Tony, who remained quiet.

The downstairs also held her father's office. "Daddy is moving out to the pool house, so this will become your new office." Tony stopped her.

"He's not staying?"

She touched his arm. "He's moving into the pool house. You will be my husband and the head of this house. My father will maintain his independence and have his own space. This house will be our space."

She pulled him by the hands up the stairs. There were four bedrooms upstairs; hers was the most modern with a private bath. "This will be Sasha's room. The mattress in relatively new and the furniture is sturdy. If she wants, or likes the furniture in any of the other rooms, we can swap out sets. I don't like mismatched though," he said as a matter of fact.

Next she pulled him to the far end of the hall. "This is the master suite." She showed him to the two large walk-in closets, the oversized master bath with Jacuzzi tub and separate shower. He loved the his-and-her water closets. "But this furniture has to go. I hate the mirrored head board."

Tony finally started to smile. "I actually like it. I can see my lovemaking face when I am taking you on a trip to Smileyville," he said as he gnawed on his bottom lip, while pumping his hips.

"Whatever!" she laughed.

His eyes were on the California king size bed. "That is a big ass bed!"

"Yeah, my parents had planned for four children, but

my father's career took off and my mother took ill, so ..." she said with some melancholy in her voice.

"Which side of the bed do you prefer?" he asked her as he fiddled with her hair.

"I prefer the side closest to the bathroom," she said as her breath caught. He was standing so close.

"And I like the side closest to the door," he said as he lowered his head and nibbled on her neck.

Jennifer pulled away. "If you don't stop, we will never get through all the things we need to get cleared up today."

His hands slid down her waist to rest on her butt. "I know, but it has been a week. I want you so bad I can barely concentrate on what you're saying."

"Let's head downstairs. I think the bed is making it hard for you to focus," she told him as she pulled away.

"No, looking at the bed is making me hard for you," he waggled his brows.

It took a bit of finesse, but she managed to get him down the stairs to the kitchen, where she made him some tea. There were lots of details to discuss, especially with school starting in a little over a month. Sasha would be starting high school in the fall, and paperwork had to be done to get her enrolled in a new school district. But Tony was distracted.

"Jen, I, um, got a job offer as a project manager for a graphic design firm. I would be making a lot more and guaranteed good hours, in at nine, home by six. Considering the cost of upkeep on this house, as well as, I am sure, a hefty mortgage, I am going to take it," he told her.

"Tony, take the job if you want the job. There is no

mortgage on this house. My dad had solar panels installed years ago, so utilities are low. The guy who maintains the yard also takes care of the pool." She frowned a bit. "I think my dad gave him a scholarship or his firm sponsored him through school or something...." She was still frowning. "My father does not pay full price for anything!"

This made Tony feel a lot better. "What about you? What have you decided about your restaurant and what is next for you?"

"I want to sell it," she said.

"You sure?"

Her eyes were wide. "Yes, I am sure. I have been a certified chef since I was 20 years old. I have been stuck in a kitchen for 13 years. I am over it. Waaayyy over it. I have a few ideas I wanted to run by you."

"I'm listening," he said. By the end of her lists of ideas, Tony was so turned on he was afraid to stand for fear of snapping off his children maker. Her list started with combining their honeymoon with a family vacation for the three of them to Orlando. This included bringing along Emily, Sasha's best friend, to share a hotel room and someone for the teen to hang with at Universal Studios.

Her list also included two new business ventures. The first was a line of natural seasoning combinations of sea salt and herbs. "I was thinking, in the summer time, on weekends, we could rent an RV and maybe hit some southern food festivals like the Chittlin' Strut or the Alabama Shrimp Festival and get a booth. I can also sell the seasonings to local small restaurants." She asked him to design a logo.

The second idea he thought was even more brilliant

than the first. "You know, I thought about Ebony and her inability to cook. I mixed that idea with Sasha and her desire to want to eat healthy. I am going to combine the two." She told him about her website idea to have Sasha maybe do two online cooking demonstrations per month via video of simple but classy dishes with few ingredients.

"We will have recipes, tutorials and merchandise, which is where we will make the money. I want to call it the Savvy Teen," she told him.

Tony's mind was reeling. "You are going to do all of this?"

"Yes. I am ready to be a wife and mom. I am ready to have some babies. I can run these two simple businesses from the house, be home when Sasha gets out of school, all the while burping Anthony, Jr.," she said with a coy wink.

He was more than ready to start making his son. His body told her so when he stood up. "Jennifer, kiss me and tell me you love me."

"I love you Tony P," she told him as she kissed him.

Slowly, he pulled away from her embrace, and took a small box from his back pocket. He took to one knee. "Jennifer Marie Taylor, I cannot imagine a more perfect wife. Will you do me the honor of consenting to be my wife and share the rest of our lives together?" He opened the box to reveal a stunning half-carat pink diamond that sparkled like the sun on a crystal chandelier.

Her eyes were full of tears as she said yes. "Tony, anytime ... any place ... any moment of the day or night, I will be yours."

"Good, get over here and kiss me with yo' fine ass," he said as he slipped the ring on her finger.

Neither could have imagined a random meeting in a bar could have led to this. Tony P was the right man for Jennifer and he knew his prayers had been answered. Jennifer had created the perfect menu for loving him and his daughter.

Epilogue... Coffee & Liquor

The wedding was small and took place in July in Tony's family church, but was officiated by the Rev. Willie Hammonds, Jennifer's pastor, who had also baptized her as a child. Johnny walked her down the aisle as Ebony, Cleo and Sasha served as her maids of honor and Gloria the matron of honor. Katie Mae wore a dress to the church that was inappropriately cut too low and sent the women in the church into a tizzy and the menfolk in one as well.

Tony's groomsmen were his brother Tino, Waldo and Domini, who had taken to calling him Unk. Raheem served as the best man. A best man who was upset that the wedding was in the middle of the afternoon and there was no live band, or dancing because the reception was in the basement of the church.

It was fine with Jennifer, who much like her husband, didn't believe in a great deal of waste, which also meant the two decided to forgo a bridal shower since between their two homes, they had more than they needed. Tony's home became a rental property and the perfect place for Katie Mae to raise Raja and Domini. The small amount of excess from the rent they paid took care of the mortgage and the rest was placed into a college fund for Sasha.

That money was needed because the four years sped by. Sasha was accepted to Le Cordon Bleu in Paris. As Tony was packing up one child to head off to college, Jennifer was packing up their son to start pre-K. Anthony, Jr. looked a great deal like his father, but his sister, Dianna, was a small replica of her mother. A darling little girl who had her father wrapped around her finger and turned her grandfather into a baby talking babbling idiot.

Tony, who was happy to be out of the house and working alongside people, absolutely flourished in his new job. He was promoted to Senior Project Manager in less than two years and made Junior Vice President in less than four. The special dinners at his home with he and his wife were coveted invitations that his employees worked hard to earn. The summer pool parties at their home were like a social event of the season. Especially when people found out that his father-in-law was Johnny Taylor, one of the most noted attorneys in Atlanta.

Johnny began working part time with Gloria on several projects and was out of the house at least four days a week and Wednesdays were still his golf day. His hunting days became less frequent as the arthritis made it hard for him to stay out in the cold for long periods of time. Tony bought an RV that he would take out to gaming sites so that he and his father-in-law could get in at least a few hunting days together. It was the same RV they used on the weekends in the summer to hit the road for food festivals, where Jennifer sold out of her sea salt spices. The most noted one was the lavender and lemongrass, which she also had made into a creamy lotion and body scrub that women loved. This one she called grasses of lavender.

And as for Jennifer, she could not be happier. Once a week, she would have Jacqueline over to help out with the babies, even though she didn't need it. Upon hearing her mother-in-law singing one evening to Anthony, Jr., she inquired about her vocal abilities. Once she told Jennifer she had wanted to be a singer, Jennifer made a few phones calls.

As an early Christmas present, she got a sitter for the kids and drove her mother-in-law over to a bare bones looking building. Inside was a music studio that handled many of the Atlanta-based artists for Arista records. Jacqueline recognized the famous artist and his babyface as he asked her to get in the booth to get a level check on her voice. Jennifer had contacted the first client she started out with who owned the hip hop record label, that Tony had did some work for as well, and got her mother-in-law a gig singing backup on a couple of jazz singers' Christmas albums.

All in all, she was happier than she had ever been. Especially when she learned to let go and understand that there is no perfect recipe for a happy life. If anything, the best we can hope is to create well-rounded courses for a menu for loving.

- Fin —

I hope you enjoyed this Slivers of Love Book. I know, I know, if it did not have the heat you were expecting, don't worry, I have some more goodies coming up for you.

Now Available exclusively on <u>Amazon</u>

Would you like to try the lotion Jennifer was making?

Created by the Pilgrim Soap Company

Gently scented with lemongrass, lavender and something special.

Pilgrimsoapcompany.com

Order yours today.

ABOUT THE AUTHOR

Olivia Gaines is the author of numerous best selling novellas and books including Two Nights in Vegas, A Few More Nights, and have had several number one best sellers with The Blakemore Files including Being Mrs. Blakemore and Shopping with Mrs. Blakemore.

She lives in Augusta, GA with her husband, son and snotty cat, Katness Evermean.

Connect with Olivia on her FaceBook page at http://on.fb.me/1eorEAr or her website at http://oliviagaines.com.

www.ingramcontent.com/pod-product-compliance
Lightning Source LLC
Chambersburg PA
CBHW020119180626
46812CB00006B/2664